FLIGHT OF SPARROWS

SMALL SACRIFICES SERIES
BOOK TWO

R.A. LINGENFELTER

This is a book of fiction. Names, places, characters, and events are fictitious in every regard. Any similarities to actual events and persons, living or dead, are purely coincidental. Any trademarks, service marks, product names, or named features are assumed to be the property of their respective owners, and are used only for reference. There is no implied endorsement if any of these terms are used. Except for review purposes, the reproduction of this book in whole or part, electronically or mechanically, constitutes a copyright violation.

Cover Illustration by Dreams2Media

Flight of Sparrows
Copyright © 2020 Artistry Utopia Publishing All rights reserved.

This book is dedicated to so many people. First and foremost, Steve Michels, the drummer from Foreign Figures and the rest of the band. Thank you for allowing me to use your inspiring music for the End of Crows and the creation of Flight of Sparrows. I wasn't joking when I said I wanted Cold War and Reign in the movies if it gets optioned. Sheryl, my editor along with my sister, Melissa Perry and friend Savannah Taylor. Thank you for working with my crazy, insane schedule. MY FANS! Oh my god, so many times you made me cry with gratitude! I'm so thankful you love Willow as much as I do! My fellow authors who also help support me and celebrate in my successes. You are so loved. And most importantly, Rebecca Poole with Dreams2Media. You created beauty with my covers and my interior. You are truly touched with a gift!

OTHER BOOKS BY R.A. LINGENFELTER

End of Crows: Book One
Flight of Sparrows: Book Two
Shadowgaze
Twisted Beginning

ONE

THE SMELL OF BLOOD JERKED me awake, the strong copper scent tingling my nose. I heard my scream as my mother fell, holding back my father who was trying to kill me. I sat on the side of the cot and ran a hand through my hair that I hadn't braided the night before.

It had been several weeks since the Dominion had attacked the Crow's camp but I still hadn't been able to get more than four hours sleep at a time. The memory of that night still haunted me.

"Willow, it's only two o'clock. You can get a few more hours of sleep in."

I glanced up at Finn who was laying on his side facing me, his cot the only other one in the room.

After the attack, he had insisted on being by my side. At the time I had felt grateful; this morning irritation was the only thing I felt.

"And I can get a few hours of training in too."

He swung his legs to the floor and pulled his blanket back. I rolled my eyes, frustration raising its ugly head. "I would rather train by myself, Finn. Go back to bed."

"You can't train hand to hand combat by yourself and you are an expert with the bow. So it looks like you need a partner."

I began to quickly braid my long, black hair. "Fine. Your funeral."

He was gracious enough to ignore my stinging words and I began to feel slightly guilty for snapping at him. He had been nothing but supportive since the attack.

Once we had gotten the Crows safely to the northern camp, questions began to bombard us. Finn and Duncan explained about the spies and the plan to kill us all during the meeting. The concern arose when everyone found out that my father had been one of those spies. Kathy spoke up accusingly, stating that if my father had been a spy, how could anyone be sure that I wasn't?

I hadn't had an answer for her. My thoughts and feelings were still reeling from the pain of losing my parents, and my brother, Brice, being taken by Bradlee. Finn had stood up for me, designating himself as my champion.

"You worked and practiced alongside Bradlee for over a year, Kathy. How could *you* not know he was a spy?"

She shrunk back, embarrassed and angry that he hadn't taken her side. Luckily Finn didn't allow her attack to gain any ground with the rest of the Crows. "We are all shocked. Bradlee worked beside us, ate with us and even got the Danners safely here. Kennet and Agatta had been a part of this community from the very beginning so there was no way of knowing that the Dominion had gotten into Kennet's head. I know, more than any of *you*, what intimate betrayal does to a person. I have worked *harder* than anyone here to prove to you all that I am not my mother's son. Don't do that to Willow. She's lost enough as it is."

"Ready to go?"

I looked up and saw Finn already dressed and waiting on me.

Without saying a word, I sighed heavily to let him know he wasn't welcome and I shoved past him, deliberately hitting his shoulder with mine. I knew I was asking for a fight, but if I was being honest, I wanted one.

The northern camp we had escaped to had nicer and more accommodating amenities, but it was more exposed than the mountain camp. The gym had more light, and updated equipment, including weight benches. The kitchen had all the gadgets to make any delicacy you could ever desire. Unfortunately, exhaust from using those ovens and gadgets weren't dispersed and could be easily seen from the sky and after the initial impressed reaction, I saw now why they chose the camp hidden deeper in the mountains. Part of me missed it; my first home as a free Crow.

I began my warmup taking my anger out on the hundred-pound heavy weight punching bag. My wrapped hands took on the shock and sent it through my arms. I didn't feel any of the jarring or the pain as I made the hanging cylinder swing.

"You aren't going to do anybody any good if you break your hand."

I threw a glare over my shoulder, surprised when I found him standing as close to me as he was. "And how is being holed up at this camp doing anybody any good?"

"Willow, we've talked about this. We can't go back yet, it's not safe. The Dominion will be crawling all over our camp to glean any information on us that they can."

"It's been weeks, Finn. They are long gone by now. I grew up under the Dominion. I know how they work and how they think. And every day we stay here is another day closer they come to killing Brice."

I squared in front of him, needing to expel the energy that was building within me. I felt like if I didn't do something, my body was going to physically explode, or maybe I was would go insane. Logic didn't make sense and action was the only thing that would help.

He stared at me, not saying a word. I was waiting for him to either engage in a physical fight or a verbal one; I was ready for both.

He dropped his head and ran a hand through his hair. "Fine. We will go back and see if they are still there. Just you and me. I'll tell Duncan that we are going to scout the southern area to make sure the Dominion aren't tracking us, and that we will be gone for a few days. I don't want anyone following us and exposing our location."

I felt the tension leave my body as my shoulders dropped. Finally, action.

"Just make sure you keep those keen ears alert for voices or noises. We can't afford to get caught by them."

I nodded eagerly. "Of course. I don't want to get caught either. It would keep me from saving Brice."

"I still don't know how we are going to do that, Willow."

"I'm working on it. I just need you to trust me."

He grabbed my hand and squeezed before letting it go. "I do. That's what scares me."

TWO

BY NOON WE WERE HEADING back towards the mountain Crow camp. I felt a mixture of emotions churning in my stomach, twisting and turning the butterflies that fluttered there. Would my parent's bodies still be there? Would my home still be intact? I knew the base camp had been destroyed in the explosions from the ACV bombs, but our home and our gym had all been inside the mountain. Had the constabulary gone through all of our things?

Duncan had set the self-detonators in the security cave, destroying any of our intel to keep the Dominion from confiscating it. He had a backup system that he brought with us during our escape. They wouldn't know how much we knew about them.

My thoughts went back to Bradlee and Brice. My brother was a big guy, much bigger than Bradlee so I couldn't understand how Bradlee got him away from the rest of the Crows. He would've had to have drugged him somehow. Or told him one of his family were in danger. Taking into account how big Brice was, I assumed the latter. Brice could be a jerk of a big brother, but he wouldn't let anyone mess with his family.

I felt a tingle run down my arm and slowed my ATV. Despite riding for a couple hours, I knew the tingle wasn't from the vibration of the engine. Finn pulled up beside me and cut his engine.

"What is it, Willow?"

"Something. I don't know."

We were at the edge of the trees, a large meadow opened up before us. I knew we had about five more miles to go before we hit our camp. I took a deep breath and watched the wave of the dead winter grasses. There hadn't been snow yet but you could feel and smell it in the air.

A shimmer caught my attention and I sucked in my breath as I watched a Dominion constable walk through the grasses next to the trail. He had his rifle pointed forward but was searching the ground.

"What's wrong?"

I couldn't take my eyes off of the enemy. "Can't you see him, Finn?" but even as I spoke, I saw through the soldier. The outer edges of his body wispy and flowing, like a ghost from the past. He slowly dissipated into the grasses and was gone. "He's gone."

Finn grabbed my shoulder. "Who's gone? I didn't see anyone."

"The Dominion. They were here looking for evidence that we went this way."

"How do you know?"

"I saw him looking." I turned to look at Finn and saw him staring at me incredulously. I shrugged my shoulders. "Maybe it's another gift I'm just figuring out."

"Or maybe it's a side effect of you not getting enough sleep."

I gunned my ATV forward, not bothering to wait for him.

An hour later we slowly pulled into our camp. A sob caught in my throat as I saw the blackened destruction of what had been my home. The few cabins that stood were charred black, walls fallen, roofs caved in. The courtyard where we had shared so many meals as a family was barren, the benches and tables ash below our vehicles.

We stopped and shut off the engines. We investigated the gym first, wanting to see what was still there. The boxing ring, which was closest to the door was melted on one side, its boundary ropes snapped and hanging. Walking further back I felt my heart drop as I saw my beloved archery range was destroyed. Bows were snapped and left like trash littering the floor, arrows flung about. I allowed the tears to streak silently down my cheeks as I followed Finn into the ammunition room in the back. Not surprisingly, the few guns we had to leave behind, and the ammunition were missing. The Dominion were thorough.

I heard movement from the front of the cave and I ran towards the entrance, pulling my bow and nocking an arrow. I was ready to fight.

I was met with an empty room, Finn ran up behind me, his gun pulled. I looked at him, a frown claiming its place on my face. I knew I had heard someone. He obviously hadn't heard the same noise because he kept watching me, waiting to see what we were going to do next.

Thinking that the source of the noise might have gone outside, I crept towards the entrance and glanced outside. I lowered my bow, making my way towards the courtyard, awe stealing any words that I tried to form. Surrounding me was the Dominion who had stormed our camp. Their wispy forms were playing out their actions that fateful night and I watched as one of them moved right through me. Their movements were in slow motion, so I was able to see their precise attack, advancing as one large body.

"Willow, what are you doing?"

"Can't you see them, Finn?" I waved a hand through one of the soldier's torso, the nebulous image wavering at my intrusion.

"See what? You're freaking me out."

I stumbled back as an ACV rumbled towards me, its turret swinging towards the security cave. I sucked in my breath as it fired, and the side of the mountain exploded.

"I'm watching them destroy our camp."

I had an overwhelming need to see my home and I sprinted in that direction. I didn't care if Finn was following me or not.

The door was blown off its hinges and I stepped over it. The living room was free of any fire damage, but the furniture was turned over and papers everywhere. The kitchen and the rest of the house were in similar disarray.

I carefully made my way to my room, stepping over debris and trash. My room appeared to have been hit the hardest. My mattress was standing upright in the corner opposite of my bed frame. My dresser was dumped over, the drawers strewn about. They had been looking for something. I wish I knew what.

Tears blurred my eyesight making it difficult to see anything but muddied colors of mass. I hadn't outright cried since the first night in our new camp. I had been inconsolable that night and Finn had held me for hours. He never told me to hush, that things would be okay and right now I was appreciative of that. We had no idea if things were going to be "okay", or if things would "work out".

A shimmer of light flashed on the floor by my closet and I moved towards it, knowing before I saw it what it was; Mom's dress. I yanked the debris off of it and held it up. The shoulder was burnt and the back ties were shredded, but the bodice and skirt of the dress appeared unharmed. I crumpled the fabric and pressed it to my nose. I didn't know how but it still smelled like Mom's perfume that she let me wear for my first dance.

I dropped to the floor holding the dress to my face and let the pain flow through my body. I missed her so badly. I needed her more than ever for her guidance, her strength, her compassion. I didn't have enough time with her. I had just started to learn my gifts and the questions I hadn't known to ask were here now; unanswered.

A noise in the hallway broke through my grief and I glanced up towards the doorway. A constable came flowing through the entry, tossing my mattress up against the wall, pulling drawers from my dresser out before dumping it over. His determination to find whatever he was looking for unrelenting.

The misty form looked familiar, but I was so engrossed in watching the replay of the destruction of my room that I didn't place him right away. Then he pulled his face mask down. Bradlee.

"I'm not finding anything in here."

I scrambled to my feet, clutching the dress. None of my Dominion ghosts had talked before. When he moved towards the closet, I stumbled back towards the bedroom door to get out of his way. He paused, pulled out the dress hanging in my closet that I currently held in my hands and gently touched the fabric before throwing it to the floor. He rifled through the closet, but when he didn't find the object of his search, he turned and headed back to the door, flowing right through me.

When I saw him make his way towards me, I sucked in my breath knowing he had to go through me to leave the room. I didn't know what to expect; cold chills, sensing his presence or having the wind knocked out of me. None of that happened. He just disappeared.

I left my room hoping to spot him again. If I followed him, I might find out what was so important and what he was looking for. I raced to my parents' room but finding it empty, went to Brice's room. Other than the destruction the constabulary had wreaked on it earlier, there was nothing. The ghosts of the past were gone.

I heard Finn call my name and I made my way to the front of the house. He was standing in the living room examining the destruction. His green eyes locked with mine.

"Did you find any answers?"

I shook my head. "No but Bradlee was here. He was the one who destroyed my room," I shrugged my shoulders and looked around. "and probably the rest of the house. He was looking for something but didn't find it."

Finn nodded towards the fabric still in my hand. "You found your dress?"

I suddenly felt silly for holding onto it, but couldn't let it go. The little girl inside who hadn't been given the chance to grow up like a normal child clung to it like a lost beloved stuffed animal. I couldn't bear to part with it. "It's the only thing I have left of my Mom."

He moved towards me and wrapped his arms

around my body. I stayed frozen for a moment, attempting to stay strong but I finally succumbed and gripped onto him. He was the only lifeline I had right now. I knew he would hold me for as long as I needed him to, but time was passing and we still didn't have any answers. I squeezed him tight for a second before releasing him and pulling back.

"I need to go to Dad's garage. Maybe there's something there."

He didn't say anything but nodded. We went back to our ATVs and started down the southern trail to the garage. I slowed as we passed the spot where Dad had captured me and where he and Mom had died. I felt sick in my stomach, not wanting to see their bodies but unable to look away. I knew we needed to take the time to give them a proper burial.

I stopped the ATV and stepped off, slowly moving towards the rubble and brush. Finn walked right behind me. We pressed through the brush but found nothing but blood. My parents' bodies were gone. I began searching, wondering if I might have gotten the area wrong, but the large pool of blood from when Mom slit Dad's throat was evidence that I hadn't. I stared at Finn.

"Why would they take my parents' bodies?"

"They probably didn't want the Crows to get a

hold of any PIMs. Any information we can glean from the Dominion would be considered a breach."

Anger fueled me once again. It was a feeling I had fed upon for so many weeks that it was familiar and powerful. "They had no right to take my family. And I swear if they hurt Brice at all, heaven help them." I pushed past him and jumped on my machine. I wanted answers and the need to have them now was overpowering.

I raced towards the garage, probably faster than what was safe, but I didn't care. Best case scenario was that there was something in Dad's office that would help me find the answers to my questions. As I burst through the clearing, I saw the tall shop standing silent, it's parking lot empty. I wasn't surprised. I figured the Dominion would take the ACVs when they attacked the camp. I drove around to the front of the building, stopping suddenly when a lone ACV sat by the doors. Goosebumps ran over my skin causing the hairs on the back of my neck to stand. I sat there staring at it, waiting for the giant beast to come to life or expose the life forms inside but nothing moved.

"I wonder why they left this one here?"

I jumped at Finn's voice. I had forgotten he was there. "I don't know why."

A form came around the side of the ACV and my heart jumped into my throat a second time. It was only slightly reassuring that it was a vision constable instead of flesh and bone. I watched as the he climbed up into the machine, a second soldier standing down below talking with the one inside the tank.

"It won't start."

"Try the bypass switch. That usually works."

"Nope. Nothing. It's dead."

"We will have to come back for it. We don't have time to mess with it now."

I watched as the figure climbed down from the machine and the two disappeared into the building. I stepped off my ride and moved towards the ACV. Tentatively touching it, I held my breath. Last time I had touched one of these machines it had burned my hand.

It didn't cause me any pain. Instead, I felt an alliance with the beast. I watched as constabulary milled around it like ants around a piece of food. They had come back for it, after they burned the camp. In fast motion I watched Dominion constabulary and IT work all over the behemoth trying to get it started, but the tank stayed still, no life coming from the large machine. They eventually left it, unable to move the large piece of machinery out of the mountains.

I climbed up onto the vehicle and opened the lid.

"What are you doing, Willow?"

I glanced at him. "Following my gut." I dropped down inside and moved towards the cockpit. I sat down, looking at all of the knobs and switches. The dash appeared foreign to my eyes and I wasn't sure what I was supposed to do. Taking a deep breath and closing my eyes, I hesitantly raised my right hand. I allowed my instincts to take over and my hands quickly began flipping switches. The leviathan roared to life, it's engine purring. I felt giddy and exhilarated.

I turned on the cameras and saw Finn stepping back from the machine in awe. Climbing up and popping my head outside, I grinned. "I don't think she wanted the Dominion to have her back."

"She? You are communicating with a machine?"

Shaking my head, I tried to figure out how to explain it. "It's not like I'm talking to it. I sense things. I'm seeing what happened like watching a movie. I'm not a part of it, just an observer."

I slid back down and shut the machine off. I was going to be taking this back to the Crow's camp to the north.

Climbing back outside, I dropped to the ground. "Let's go inside and see if they left anything."

We made our way into the large steel building, finding it in the same disrepair as my home had been. Furniture and papers were scattered about, firing up my anger again. The people who supported and worked for the Dominion were pushing oppression and slavery upon others. It was wrong; no way around it. I couldn't understand why people would believe the lies and give up their own rights as a human being. We were born to be free.

I walked around the room knowing we weren't going to find anything to help us fight the Dominion. We had found what had drawn me here. The ACV.

"We need to get back to camp. The only answers we are going to find are going to be inside the Dominion."

"We haven't been able to breach the Dominion city, Willow. How do you expect to get inside without being detected?"

"The Crows got my family out of there; they can get me back in."

Finn shook his head. "It's a death mission. It's one thing to get someone out and hidden, but to get you *in* and keep you hidden with all of the cameras they have? It's never been done."

"There's a first time for everything, Finn. I *have* to go back." I started walking towards the entrance but he grabbed my arm to stop me.

"Just give it a bit of time. We've asked our Crows from the south and the east to come meet up with us at camp. They will be here in just a couple of weeks."

I pulled my arm from his grasp. "I don't *have* a couple of weeks. Every day that I'm not in there is another day closer to the Dominion killing Brice. I *won't* let my brother die. They already killed my mother and father; they won't take my last family member." I stomped outside, trying to catch my breath. I knew time was running out for my brother and I couldn't understand why Finn didn't comprehend that. Although had lost his mother to the Dominion, he still had his father, Duncan. I was about to lose my entire family if I didn't do something now.

"Willow, you can't go in there by yourself. The Dominion will catch you and they will punish you. If you just wait until the Crows…"

I whirled on him, unleashing my anger and frustration. "Wait for the Crows to what? I waited last time and look at what happened. The Dominion moved in and the Crows scattered to the winds like sparrows taking flight. Scared little birds." I began to climb the ACV. "I'm not a scared little bird anymore, Finn. I'm not going to sit back and allow the Dominion to take one more life. We are not property; they do not own us."

"I know you are hurting badly and worried about Brice, but we need to bring this to the Crow council and talk about it."

I glared down at him. "I'm not a Crow anymore, Finn. I refuse to have one more organized society tell me what I can or cannot do." I dropped down into the ACV and started up the machine. It purred to life. "Alright sweet thing. Let's go back to camp."

I could see in the rear cameras that Finn was following along behind. His ATV was much faster than my ride, but he stayed with me. I felt slightly guilty for snapping at him like I did. I knew he was trying to keep me safe along, with the faction but I couldn't wait any longer. I hoped he would come around to understand my point of view. I would never put the Crows in danger; they were good people just trying to live a peaceful, *free* life. I'd die before I would expose them to Dominion rule.

The engine began to sputter in my ACV and it rolled to a stop in a silence. I opened the hatch and climbed down. Finn pulled up beside me. I scanned my beast looking for steam, smoke or any sign of where the malfunction was coming from.

"Maybe you aren't supposed to take this back to the faction."

I shook my head. "I don't understand. She was running just fine." I placed a hand on the cold steel and a wave of electricity shot through me. I walked around the tank, following a pull that was sensed only by me. Finn followed silently. We moved down a slight decline through tall aspen before breaking through to a small field. At first glance, it appeared to be a regular open meadow but some of the shapes appeared irregular. I moved towards a wall of brush for a closer inspection. The gasp that escaped my mouth was deafening in the mountain silence. The wall of brush was a camouflaged tarp covering wooden boxes.

"They've just brought this since the attack. We would've found it during our scouting if it had been here before."

I turned towards Finn. "Do you think they know where our northern camp is?"

"If my mother hadn't told them then I'm sure Bradlee has," he opened one of the cases and found two assault rifles tucked within. "I just never thought they would move so fast as to plan another attack so soon."

I ripped the tarp the rest of the way off. "Well, we can just hinder them and help ourselves. How many cases do you think we can load on top of Bernice?"

"Bernice?"

I shrugged my shoulders, feeling slightly silly and childlike. "She just feels like a Bernice to me."

He chuckled while he eyed the stash. "There's straps here so we can go wide and high. I bet we could confiscate all of them from the Dominion if we wanted to. We are going to have to make camp here though. By the time we get everything loaded and strapped it'll be dark and almost midnight before we reach camp."

"I think the group will be okay once they see the gifts we brought."

"If we don't give them a heart attack first with the ACV."

"Finn, we are running out of time. I can't explain *how* I know but I just do. We don't have the luxury of making camp. We need to get this back to camp and let the others know. If there's another camp that your mother or Bradlee didn't know about, now is the time to consider it."

The intensity of his gaze was uncomfortable but I refused to show it. I kept my gaze unwavering, silently challenging him to argue. He didn't argue but instead nodded, which I admit shocked me a bit.

"I trust you, Willow. You have gifts that I can't understand and you haven't been wrong so far. If you say we need to move then we need to move." He turned and picked up the first case. "I'll hand them up to you so we can secure them to the top of *Bernice*."

I quickly climbed up onto the ACV and within two hours we had the entire stash of weapons and ammunition loaded and secured. We had agreed that when we came within a mile of camp, I would use the radio inside the ACV to try and reach Duncan and give them a heads up that the ACV that would be rolling into camp was friendly. If I couldn't reach him, Finn would race on ahead and give them the information.

I sat back in the cockpit as Bernice roared to life. I followed Finn in the darkness, the single square light from his ATV illuminating the way. My mind was racing and my heartbeat quick while I thought about how I was going to get *back* into the Dominion. It wasn't going to be easy but I knew it would be easier than how I was going to get out, especially since another person would be with me. I would die before I would leave without Brice. Of that I had no doubt.

I had been up for twenty-four hours by the time I crawled back into my bed. It didn't take me as long to fall asleep as I had thought it would. I guess having made up my mind on how and when I was going to leave the camp eased my soul. It was the first time since the attack that I had felt at ease.

I was groggy and surprised to find I had slept ten hours. I sat up, letting my legs dangle for a moment to get the circulation flowing and work the stiffness from my limbs. A shimmer caught my attention and

I saw my dress lying across the foot of my bed. I had forgotten it inside the ACV. Finn must've brought it in for me. I stroked the soft fabric and smiled.

Standing up and stretching, I quickly got dressed and went to the courtyard to find Duncan. I would need his help getting back into the Dominion.

The sun was shining brightly and kids were running about playing. Adults were bustling back and forth getting the new camp settled and I wondered when and how we were going to tell them that this was temporary; we would have to move again and soon.

"Good afternoon, Willow!"

"Good afternoon, Jennifer." Since coming home with the spoils of the Dominion treasure and the ACV, Finn and I were heroes. The only person who still held any animosity towards me was Kathy, and I didn't expect that to change, regardless of what I did.

I found Duncan examining Bernice. "Find anything interesting?"

He grinned at me and shook his head. "It honestly makes no sense at all why it wouldn't start when the Dominion moved out. I can't find any flaws or shorts in the circuitry at all."

"That's because she was waiting for me. She knew she was supposed to help me."

"So 'she' is now a part of this Crow faction?"

I cringed when Duncan used the reference. "No. She's not a *Crow*. My grandmother was wrong to use that term. Crows are clever and smart. They teach their young all that they know. We didn't do that. We flutter about waiting for the Dominion to do something and when they do, we scatter like scared little birds."

"Sparrows is the term I think you used."

I whirled coming face to face with Finn. I placed my hands on my hips, ready to argue. "Yes, like little sparrows. We keep letting them take the upper hand."

"And how do you propose to take back that upper hand?"

I hated that I didn't have an answer for him. It was a legitimate question. "I don't know but having rebels scattered everywhere instead of coming together doesn't help anyone. We need to bring everyone together."

Duncan stood up. "A movement that large will alert the Dominion and bring attention to ourselves."

"Aren't you tired of hiding, Duncan?"

"You haven't been a part of the rebels long enough to know what we have been dealing with," Finn snapped.

I glanced at Finn. "No. I've only been *inside* the Dominion to know what's going on. Every day hearing of families torn apart because of a debt that's owed by the parents. Men and women who lose their kids if they screw up with them just once, or who have become hooked on drugs; drugs that the Dominion provided in the first place. Forced to have tracking chips implanted into your jaw to keep you under control, never knowing if or when *they* decide your life is no longer important," I swiped at my jaw line where the faint scar ran up to my ear lobe, anger and frustration running rampant. "knowing that the value of your life is based on how well you behave and produce for an evil entity that sees you only as chattel."

He couldn't look me in my eyes and averted them towards the ground between us which only fueled my anger. They were still living under Dominion rule, they just didn't know it. Fear still dictated how they moved, breathed, participated in this life. It was just in a different location. Why couldn't they see that?

I took a deep breath. Fighting with them wouldn't make them see. I needed to explain my position better. "The Dominion keep us scattered because it's easier to control us. If we were to come together, we are a force to be reckoned with. There's *never* going to be a good time because they keep us scattered for a reason. We need to take the reins and control our future."

Duncan scratched the back of his head. "And how

do you propose to do that?"

"I need identification. I need to be someone important enough to move around but not so important that I attract attention. I was thinking a family welfare inspector."

Finn shook his head. "I've never heard of them."

"They move about making sure that parents are taking care of their kids properly. If they see something they don't like, they take the kids."

"They take them from the parents?"

I nodded. "Yep. It's a pretty common occurrence."

Duncan stared at me and I was internally preparing for an argument. but his warm brown eyes softened from their previous sharpness. "Okay. Give me a few days and I'll see what I can do."

I nodded and smiled; it felt alien on my face. "Thanks, Duncan."

THREE

THE STANDARD BLACK SUV ROLLED to a stop in front of my old home. I shouldn't have stopped here but I couldn't resist. I wanted to see my home of seventeen years.

The windows were dark and there was no sign of life inside which surprised me slightly. Usually the Dominion didn't waste any time before filling in holes. Even the small a contribution my family made left a small hole. Of course, it was five o'clock in the morning, its occupants may still be inside asleep.

I pulled around to the alley and drove to the back of the house. The trash cans were empty and the backyard gate was open slightly. I pulled into the parking space and turned off the engine. Maybe I should just look around a bit, it could be a place to stay while I found Brice.

I took the keys out of the ignition before opening the door to prevent any sound. Clicking the driver's door shut, I glanced around again before walking up to the back door. It was also slightly open and I felt the hairs go up on the back of my neck. Someone had been here.

I shook my head. Of course someone had been here. The constabulary had probably been all over the house trying to find any clues as to how we escaped, and if we left any evidence as to our whereabouts. I pulled out the small flashlight from my pants pocket and clicked it on. The laundry room was basically untouched so I moved on towards the kitchen. There were some papers on the dining room table and I moved towards them. They were assessment reports from when Brice and I had gone to Dominion education. I think Mom called them report cards in her day. Nothing else in the kitchen was out of place.

I quietly moved towards my bedroom and pushed the door open. Where everything was in its place in the other two rooms, my room was just the opposite. Things had been turned over and scattered about. My uniforms, the mattresses on my bed, my closet, even my dresser was lying about in pieces. They had definitely been looking for something, but what?

"Over here. I think I found something."

I whirled, my heart beating in my throat. I saw a shadow move across the doorway and I slunk down, hoping to blend in with the rubble.

A towering constable slammed open my door and came charging in.

I stood, realizing it was a memory shimmer like what I had seen in the valley with Finn. I watched in fascination as he and another constable trashed my room, looking for something. He was the biggest soldier I had ever seen, built like a mountain. His blonde hair was almost the color of snow it was so light, which made his piercing blue eyes look like glaciers. There was no sign of kindness or compassion in them. They were as cold as steel.

With each drawer, box and paper that he searched and then tossed away, his frustration grew. It was apparent with how aggressive he became at each dead end. He shoved past the other constable and with a yell, flipped over the mattresses on my bed. Pulling out a knife, he shredded the fabric to see if there were any treasures hidden inside.

Despite knowing he was just a vision of the past, I shuddered and kept out of his way. He was definitely one that I needed to stay away from.

He stomped out the door and moved towards Brice's bedroom. I followed but he had disappeared along with the other shimmers. I crept to Brice's bedroom and found his room in the same condition, along with my parents.

I didn't think they would find anything. We had kept our noses and our lives pretty clean as we prepared to escape to Crow's camp. We didn't want any evidence of our intentions had the Dominion decided to raid our home before then.

I padded my way to the living room, trying to figure out what they had been looking for. I didn't see the figure sitting on the couch until he spoke.

"We've been waiting for you. Thought you could sneak back in and not have the Dominion know?"

I squeaked as the air I sucked in lodged in my throat. This wasn't a shimmer.

As the figure stood, I realized it was the icy mountain who I had seen trash my room just moments earlier. He pointed his rifle at me and I slowly raised my hands.

"I'm supposed to bring you in for questioning since your brother hasn't cracked."

"Brice is still alive?" I felt relief flood my body. My brother was still alive.

"He is, but not for long. You and your family have

made a mockery of the Dominion. You *will* tell us where the compound is in Montana."

"What?" I tried to unscramble the millions of thoughts in my head. "I don't know where the camp in Montana is. I only know of the one the Dominion destroyed."

He took a step towards me. "I don't believe that. Your brother was with the Crow's IT security. He isn't cracking but maybe if he sees his little sister, he'll sing like a canary."

Anger gave me courage and I stepped towards him. "He'll never crack, you asshole. Just like I won't either."

"Well, if you aren't going to be any help, then…"

He fired his rifle and I felt burning radiate out through a sharp pain in my gut. I clenched my stomach as he laughed. When I looked down, I saw blood seeping through my clothes and my fingers. I knew I was in shock because I couldn't formulate any words. I took a step towards him pulling out my throwing knife. I threw it so fast he barely had time to register but the blood made my fingers slip and it lodged in his shoulder above his heart instead of stopping the beating black muscle within.

"You bi…" He aimed the rifle at my head and pulled the trigger.

I gasped, sitting up quickly, sweat dripping down my back despite the chilling fall temperatures outside. I jumped up and ran through the camp, searching for Duncan. I found him at his desk in the IT building.

"Willow, what's wrong? You look like you've seen a ghost."

"They know I'm coming. They are expecting me back."

"How do you know that?"

"I dreamt it, just like I did when they attacked the mountain camp." I quickly ran down what happened in my vision, Duncan listening intently.

"Then you can't go."

I jumped, not realizing Finn was behind me. "I have to go. They have Brice and he's alive," I turned back towards Duncan. "They want to know where the Crow's camp is in Montana." I saw Duncan blanche and I knew then that it was true; there was a camp in Montana.

"They know about the camp then?"

"What camp? I thought ours was the largest."

Finn moved up beside me. "No, the one in Montana is the largest. We didn't think anyone in the Dominion knew about it. The technology protecting it is even more advanced than the Dominion's."

Duncan was staring at Finn. "We need to let them know."

I shook my head. "They don't know *where* it is. They've been torturing Brice to get it out of him, but he hasn't cracked."

Duncan shook his head. "Because he doesn't know about it. There are only a handful of us who know about it; to keep its secret."

"I'll send Quinn to let them know and to prepare." Finn spoke to Duncan. I felt slightly irritated that I was being kept out of the conversation.

"Didn't you hear me? They are torturing Brice and they won't stop until they have that information or he's dead."

Finn turned to me. "All the more reason for you to stay and let others go back to get Brice. They will use Brice against you and make you crack. We just can't take that risk. There are too many other lives at stake, Willow."

I stepped closer, glaring at him. "You don't think I know that? *Both* of my parents died because of me but I still sacrificed everything to make sure the Crow faction would be safe. Brice is the only family I have left, and I'm *not* going to sit around and wait for others to decide his fate," I whirled towards Duncan. "You said only a handful of people know about the camp in Montana and that's the information they want. Don't tell me anymore about it. Then if I'm caught, they can torture me all they want but I won't be able to tell them anything because I won't know," I shot a nasty look towards Finn. "Problem solved."

Without waiting for an answer, I left them and headed towards my room. I wasn't going to wait another minute. Time was critical, yet neither one of them seemed to understand that. I began slamming supplies into a knapsack.

"Do you really think you are going there by yourself?"

I started but I didn't turn to face Finn. I didn't want him to see the emotions on my face and give away how vulnerable I felt at that moment. I needed to allow myself that moment because once I walked out of the Crow's camp, I had to depend on my anger to fuel me. Weakness was not an option.

I felt his hand on my arm, stilling my movement. Taking a deep breath, I turned to face him. His green eyes searched mine and I felt my resolve crumble. He just wanted to keep me safe, like I wanted to keep Brice safe.

"Willow, I'm trying to help."

"By keeping me here, trapped, just like the Dominion did for the past eighteen years of my life? I'm done having people tell me what to do. We escaped for freedom, remember?"

"I understand, but going back in there is a suicide mission. If you talked to this constable, maybe he has the same gift that you do and he knows your coming. Then we'd have to gather an undercover recovery group to get you back, which would lead to another battle that the Crows aren't quite ready for."

I clenched my fists. "And *why* aren't the Crows ready? You've had over seventeen years to prepare. Why haven't the Crows retaliated? Why do you keep to the shadows and live in fear?"

Finn looked over my head, his eyes unfocused. "We've lost so many people. The war was hard on families and lives were lost. I guess we became comfortable being able to live the way we could in seclusion."

"I know it's a huge sacrifice, but you are still living under the Dominion rule. Your every move is determined by whether or not they can find you. You are still living in fear."

He looked into my eyes and took a deep breath. "Are you sure you just turned eighteen?"

I sighed deeply. It felt like that night had been years ago. "Yep. You were my first dance at my birthday party, remember?"

"How could I forget? I was dancing with the prettiest girl in the camp."

The butterflies in my stomach took flight and I felt them spread throughout my body, causing the muscles in my arms and legs to become unsteady. He was staring at me intensely and I knew if he didn't say something, I was going to start laughing maniacally from the tension.

I saw his head dip towards mine and I sucked in a breath. Closing my eyes, I waited nervously for my first kiss. I can't say I hadn't thought about it with Finn. Honestly with Bradlee too before I found out he was the spy. I'm glad it was going to be with Finn.

I felt his breath on my lips, like strands of spider webs brushing across my skin and goosebumps skittered through my body.

"Let me come with you, Willow."

I snapped my eyes open, finding his on mine. Stepping back embarrassed, I shoved his chest back. He was playing me, and I didn't like the way it felt. "Two of us are going to be harder to sneak back in. Plus, you aren't familiar with inside the Dominion compound. I know where cameras and security are. You are more of an impediment than a help."

I saw the pain shoot through Finn's eyes. While a part of me was satisfied that I stung him as much as he stung me when I thought he was going to kiss me, I also felt slightly guilty.

He took another step back, dropping his sight to the ground that now separated us like a canyon. "And how are you going to get Brice out if he's hurt? You told me yourself this other soldier confirmed that they've been torturing him to get information out of him. And that's another thing; he's waiting for you. You think you're really going to sneak in there and they won't be expecting you? You are putting the entire camp in danger with your risky expedition."

His tone set me off. "I'm not going to put *anyone* at risk, so let's make that clear right up front. I'll make sure I'm not followed when I bring my brother back to the camp. I won't expose the compound and the people."

When his eyes met mine, I couldn't help the shiver that ran up my spine. They were cold, just like they had been the first day we met in the forest after our escape. "No, you won't. I'll make sure of that." He turned and left the room.

Part of the old Willow wanted to run after him, to apologize for being such a witch. I didn't want to ruin our friendship or what it was turning into, but flashes of my parents' dead eyes, their life blood pooling around their bodies while I was helpless to do anything came crashing back and the pain shoved out any other emotion. I would die before I would allow

Brice to be tortured another day. The feeling that I was running out of time kept my adrenaline on high speed and I needed to get to him...*now*.

FOUR

I WAS TEMPTED TO TAKE MY ACV but knew it would announce my arrival instead of allowing me the ability to sneak back in. I settled on an OHV just in case Brice was injured and couldn't walk far. I had tentative plans on how I was going to accomplish all of this, and I figured I would work out the smaller details on my way back to the Dominion.

As I was crossing the courtyard, Duncan came running up to me. "Willow! Wait up."

I stopped and crossed my arms. I wasn't in the mood to argue with him about going. "I need to get going, Duncan."

"I know you do. I thought I could make your

trip a little easier," he smiled warmly and I relaxed a little.

"How?"

"I reprogrammed your chip. Your new name is Suzie Sun. You're a social worker coming in from Arizona. You'll be working under Bernadette Winters during your internship for the next two weeks. They are expecting you today."

I couldn't formulate any logical words. He created an identity for me within twenty-four hours and got me a legitimate way into the Dominion's compound.

When he saw I was speechless, he began laughing. "You're welcome, Willow. And there's a black SUV waiting for you down by the road. It's also programmed for you. I can help you get in but getting out is going to be up to you. I'll try and keep tabs on the SUV and your PIM so if you get Brice sooner, we will try to help you get back out. I can't make any promises. There's so many variables that I couldn't plan for all of them."

"Thank you, Duncan," I hugged him tightly. I could see why Brice gravitated towards him like a father figure. He was warmer and kinder than our own father had been. "I'll try to be back before the two weeks, and I promise I won't compromise the Crows."

"Don't you mean the Sparrows?"

I scrunched my face, feeling guilty for insulting my new family. "About that, I'm really sorry I..."

"Don't be. We have been in hiding. We have become complacent in our anonymity and all things change. Maybe this was the wakeup call we needed."

I took a deep breath. I hadn't even been with these people for a year and already they were making changes because of me. I wasn't sure if that was a good thing or not. I smiled at him and nodded my head. "Maybe so. I have to go now. I promise Brice and I will be back as soon as possible."

"Be safe, Willow."

I skipped down the path towards the parking area where the SUV would be waiting to take me back into enemy territory. Once I reached the vehicle, I slid behind the wheel and started the engine. It purred to life. Instead of pulling out right away, I stared at the path that I had just come down hoping to see Finn. We hadn't parted on good terms and I didn't like it, but I couldn't leave Brice there. Why couldn't he understand that?

I flipped through the file folder that was sitting on the passenger seat. It had a letter explaining my credentials, the address of the house I was going to be staying at and where I was going to be working. The travel card was sitting in the ashtray. I knew I was stalling, hoping that maybe Finn had changed his mind and wanted to say goodbye.

I didn't see any shadows or indications that someone was coming down the path. I just had to accept that Finn wasn't coming down to greet me, stop me or even say goodbye. I put the vehicle in reverse and turned it around. It was time to go back.

❧❦

The path took me farther north than where our family had left our SUV which had aided in our escape. When I finally reached the highway, it was beyond the cliffs where we had hidden. Driving down the paved highway, I came to the area where we had ditched the vehicle and climbed into the crevices. There wasn't an SUV or any indication that something major had transpired there. I don't know why I was expecting it to; maybe because it had been such a huge part of my life.

I continued driving until I could see the large concrete wall looming in the distance. My heart picked up its pace and I tried to calm my nerves. What if Finn was right? What if I got caught and Brice ended up dying anyways? Was I really prepared? Could I do this? I was just an eighteen-year-old girl who didn't know squat.

"Stop it, Willow."

I closed my eyes for a second as my mother's voice filled my head.

"You are a Crow. You come from strong stock who have abilities others don't have. You can best anyone with a bow and arrow, your sword skills are beyond others and you still have talents you haven't even tapped into yet. Trust your heritage, trust your heart and don't let your head get in the way."

"I miss you, Momma. I'm scared and hurt and angry. What if I can't get Brice out? What if I get caught?"

"Stop the gibberish and focus on what needs to be done. Your soul already knows what to do. Just allow it and don't get distracted. I love you, Willow."

"Mom, don't go. I need you."

I waited for her response, longed for it, but I didn't hear her again. I don't know if it was my imagination or if I had really heard her but it was the reminder I needed. A Danner never gives up.

When I reached the gate, I pulled the card that Duncan created for me and slid it through the reader. I hadn't realized I had been holding my breath until the pad flashed green and the large gates began to open. Taking a deep breath, I accelerated and watched the mammoth gates close behind me. There was no going back now; the Dominion knew I was coming.

I drove across town. My new house was on the opposite side of the city where I had grown up. I had to fight the temptation to drive by our old home before heading to my new residence. There were eyes and ears everywhere and the memory of my latest vision kept me on course. I pulled up in front of the drab, ranch style house and cut the engine. There were no purple rose bushes in the front, nothing to make it different from the other homes on the block. It was a roof over someone's head as they went through their daily routine.

I grabbed my bag I had flung in the backseat, my folder and keys from the ignition. Walking up the sidewalk, I didn't glance around. I wanted to look as if I belonged there despite the feelings inside telling me to run. I opened the door and stepped inside. It didn't smell stale, like it had been sitting empty for a while. Instead there was a fresh, lemony scent in the air and the interior actually felt warm and inviting. Walking towards the kitchen, I could almost swear that I was walking in my old home. It was silly because *all* of the homes had the same layout. Nothing differed except what you hung on the walls or the furniture you used.

The kitchen was the same as ours, minus all of the little things that had made our kitchen warmer. A piece of paper was lying on the middle of the table.

I picked it up and read it.

Good day, Suzie Sun. We are pleased to hear of your internship here at the Western Dominion campus. We will expect you at the main Social Services building at eight a.m. sharp tomorrow. Please bring your letter of credentials. Sincerely, Bernadette Winters, Director of Western Dominion Collectivism's Socialism Services.

I set the letter back down and walked through the rest of the house. In the master bedroom I found clean sheets sitting on the king-sized bed and new uniforms hanging in the closet. I pulled the clothing from the closet and moved them into the bedroom that had been mine in the other house. I couldn't bring myself to stay in the other room. It should've been my parents'.

I quickly made the bed up in the smaller room and unpacked my bag. Buried down on the bottom, I found a small package with black writing on the plain brown paper. *Take to bathroom before opening.*

I took a deep breath and grabbed my entire duffle bag, heading into the bathroom. Because all of the houses were the same, I knew exactly where all of the cameras where at. I didn't need to look. Once I was in the bathroom and had shut the door, I opened the package. Several gadgets fell out and I opened the folder paper. Recognizing Duncan's handwriting, I couldn't stop the smile. I had my new family with me.

Willow, I hope this finds you safe. Inside are the buffers that will make the cameras and microphones stop working. You need to allow the cameras to record during the day occasionally when you are home. Once our software has recorded you in all of the rooms, it will automatically create your day for you and will show you doing normal activities when you are supposed to be at the house. This should give you the freedom to go and find Brice. The hours you are supposed to be at the house, from five p.m. to seven-thirty a.m. is your free time. I'll have the recordings showing you making supper, watching television and sleeping. Stay safe and both of you come home to us.

My mind began to race. I would have to be careful when I was out but this gave me a huge advantage that I hadn't factored in. I could leave the house at night. Digging further into the box I found several more card keys with notes on them. One was for a cleaning person in the Dominion Holding facility. Another was marked as Superiority Officer for the social and community offices. I had to be careful with these cards. If they were found on my person, I'd be taken into custody and punishment would be swift and sure.

Engaging the electronic device Duncan gave me, I

took the duffle bag back into my room and set it on my bed. I needed to eat and get some sleep before I set out after dark. That should give the software plenty of time to record everything that appeared normal. No one needed to know how abnormal this night was about to get.

It was ten o'clock at night when I decided to head out. I hadn't been able to get any sleep; my senses jumping at every noise or car that drove by. Grabbing a quick bite, I dressed in the Dominion uniform and made my way out to the SUV.

Duncan hadn't said anything about the programming in the vehicle being limited so I hoped that meant that it would be under the Dominion radar. I wanted to scout out the Holding Facilities building tonight. It would make sense that they held Brice there. I would have plenty of time to investigate the social building tomorrow when I went to work.

I climbed into the front seat and shut the door, glancing over my shoulder to make sure my weapons were still in the back seat. A blanket covered the bow and arrows, but the tip of my sword glinted in the light that spilled from the street lamp. That cool steel eased the tension in my body, and I longed to hold it in my hands again. I felt strong and powerful with it in my hands; my bow slung across my shoulder. I wished there were some way I could keep them on me but with eyes everywhere, I would alert the constabulary immediately.

I started the vehicle and headed into town, pleased when I found the main social services building just a few blocks from where my temporary housing was. I circled the block, paying attention to the entrances and any exits in the building. Circling one more time, I glanced to the left and realized that the holding building was right next door.

The hairs on my arms stood on end and I wondered if Brice was in there right now, trying to figure out how to get home. The irrational part of me wanted to storm the doors and rescue my brother but I would be stopped before I even stepped through the gates. I had to be cunning, not aggressive.

Circling this building, I also took note of entrances and exits. I wanted to be prepared if we had to make a run for it, to know what doors led to freedom. Around the back of the building was a small parking lot that held quite a few vehicles. I assumed this was the worker entrance. Since I had the cleaning badge, this would be the easiest way for me to gain access to the building. I parked in the shadows across the street and watched the entrance.

The door opened and a mountain of a man came walking out. The parking lot lamp illuminated his face and my stomach clenched in a queasy grip. It was the blonde man in my dream who had shot me in my old home. I slid down further in the seat, my heart beating so loud I feared he would hear it and find me. My fear amplified when he stopped suddenly and began to look around like he was searching for something.

Though his eyes were hooded in shadow, I could imagine those piercing cold eyes tracking my location. Even if he saw my SUV, he wouldn't be able to see me. I had parked in the shadows and the cab of my vehicle was black. It didn't stop the terror I felt when his eyes landed on my SUV. I held my breath waiting. If he charged my SUV, I would be forced to defend myself but it would also force me to give up my quest. I would have to flee the Dominion territory without my brother.

He stood frozen; staring. I couldn't take my eyes off of him waiting to see what he would do. Finally, he continued walking towards his vehicle. He climbed in, started his truck and left, turning away from where I was parked. The breath I released was shaky. For the first time since Brice had been taken, I doubted myself. Who was I to take on a rescue mission? Alone?

I started the engine and slowly drove home. Maybe

Finn had been right. I was over my head and didn't know what I was doing.

I pulled into the driveway and shut off the engine. I had a decision to make and I had to make it before morning. I could leave tonight, give up this insane notion that I could save my brother, or I could continue on, start my "job" tomorrow and begin figuring out how to get Brice out.

Climbing out, the glint of steel caught my eye again and I opened the passenger rear door. I touched it softly, the cold metal soothing my soul. Wrapping my weapons in the black blanket, I decided I was going to take them into the house. They brought me comfort and I needed all I could get right now.

Arms full, I struggled slightly as I opened the door, angling my stuff through the door. Kicking the door shut with my foot, I placed my bundle onto the couch and knelt before it. Gently unwrapping it, I pulled out my bow and set it on the coffee table. The leather quiver that held my arrows was hooked on the black blanket and I struggled to get it free. Tugging a little harder, I saw that it wasn't part of the blanket, it was a separate article of material. I stood, pulling the fabric up with me.

The cloak was a soft black with a dark lavender edging. Upon closer inspection, I found that it was reversible, the deep lavender fabric just as soft as the black. I swung it over my shoulders and put it on. The hood was deep and when pulled forward, hid my face in darkness. It hung down almost to my calves with beautiful crystals embellishing the bottom. Lacing across the chest kept the fabric tight against my breast, making it easy to strap the quiver to my back.

I sat down and hugged myself. I know who had this made for me and it caused the guilt to flood my soul again. Finn. All he ever wanted to do was to keep me safe, but I was too stubborn to allow him. And who was I to think that I could do this without his help? He had been a Crow all of his life, after all. I had just been embraced into the faction recently, learning my gifts and honing my skills for less than a year. Why had I *ever* thought that I could do this alone?

Once again, my mother's voice came back to me and I remembered what she told me. I had talents that I hadn't even realized or tapped into, yet. She told me that *she* knew I could do this. I was the only one who could save Brice.

I stood up and rubbed the edging along the cloak. I had so many people who believed in me and thought I could do this. I needed to believe in myself too.

Taking off the cloak, I folded it gently and placed

it back into the blanket. I would keep it hidden in my room for now. I could use it at night, slipping through the shadows to find out where Brice was. Until then, I needed to get some sleep and start my new job tomorrow.

FIVE

I WAS AWAKE BEFORE DAWN, NERVOUS spiders crawling through my stomach and across my skin. I was dressed and ready for the first day of the first job I'd ever had. It was kinda crazy to think about because I had never dreamed that I would be eighteen years-old and working for the Dominion under a false name. I didn't think I'd be behind Dominion walls at all at this age.

I started giggling thinking about the irony and trying to calm the nerves that continued to spin their web. Grabbing a pastry from a basket on the counter, I nibbled on it as I wandered the house. If I closed my eyes, I could almost imagine that it was our house.

Twelve steps from the kitchen doorway to my room. Six steps to the bathroom and twenty to Mom's and Dad's room. That was the only similarity. There were no marks on the doorway into the kitchen marking each year's growth for Brice and I. There was no hole in the hallway wall where Brice and I were wrestling and he accidently put his hand through the wall. There were no purple roses along the front walkway.

I glanced around wondering how I missed the fresh paint smell before. Someone had lived here; before me. Had it been another family? Had they marked their child's or children's growth on the wall like we did? Had that family shared love and laughter under this roof? Had they been torn apart too?

I dropped the pastry into the trash, disgust filling my body. If I had ever had any doubt as to whether or not I belonged here, it vanished like a specter. I hated it here. I hated the oppression, the dictatorship and suffering that the Dominion ruled with. I needed to focus on locating Brice and getting the both of us out of here and back to the Crow's camp. I slipped on the drab, gray business uniform assigned to me and studied myself in the mirror. The jacket fit a little snug but the slacks and white cotton shirt were my size. I checked my jacket and found a small pen and pad of paper tucked into the inside pocket of the cotton material. I only wondered for a moment about who the person was before me who had worn this. Were they still alive? Shaking my head, I wanted to flush the dread I felt in my body. I had to be on my game today.

Climbing into the SUV, I made my way to the CSS building. Maybe Bernadette would be impressed that I was early.

Pulling up to the parking lot, a constable came out from his booth and stopped me.

"What business do you have here?"

I swallowed nervously. "I start my new job today. I'm supposed to meet with Bernadette Winters."

"Do you have your credentials?"

I closed my eyes and groaned internally. I was supposed to bring the letter, but I forgot it on the kitchen table. I opened my eyes and smiled at him sheepishly. "I forgot it on the kitchen table. I can run home really fast and grab it. I just hate being late on my first day and I don't know how nice Ms. Winters is."

Surprisingly I saw his eyes soften. "You don't want to be late on your first day with Ms. Winters. She can be a bear," he pulled out a scanner. "I'll just scan your PIM this time."

My heart leapt into my throat and I felt panic flood my body. I don't think Duncan had covered for this and I really didn't want the side of my face blown off my first full day of reconnaissance. "That's okay, I'll just run back…"

He pulled his scanner back and smiled. "See how fast and painless that was? Go on in Miss…," he glanced at his scanner again, "Sun. This will be our little secret."

I tittered nervously, holding back the urge to scream in relief. Obviously, Duncan had planned for the PIM's and had mine reprogrammed. "Thank you, sir. Have a nice day." I drove into the parking lot and found an empty spot. Turning off the engine, I rested my head against the steering wheel. I needed to get myself together.

Taking a deep breath, I made my way towards the three-story brick building. The mirrored glass of the windows reflected a tall, confident young woman, far from what I was feeling inside. I pushed the door open and walked boldly towards the reception desk. A dark-haired brunette sat behind the counter, typing on the surface keyboard. She barely glanced up at me.

"May I help you?"

"I'm here to meet with Bernadette Winters."

She looked me up and down, disdain in her eyes. "Ms. Winters is a very busy woman. Do you have an appointment?"

Holding back irritation, I looked back at her with

the same distain. "I should hope so. I'm her intern for the next few weeks. Shall I explain to her why I'm late on my first day?"

I saw the brunette's eyes widen and she sat up straighter. "You must be Suzie Sun. Yes, she's been expecting you. Take the elevator up to the third floor and her office is at the end of the hall. I will let her know you are coming, Suzie."

"Thank you, and it's Miss Sun." I walked away without looking back and prayed I looked as confident as I sounded. I needed to show that I wasn't someone who could be walked over. I wanted to establish my dominance immediately like a wolf in a pack; I needed to show that I was the alpha.

I pushed the elevator button and waited, facing the doors and with my back straight. When they finally opened, I stepped inside and hit the floor button. I knew there were cameras in the elevator; they were everywhere, so I didn't release my pent-up breath all at once. I knew she would see that. As the motors engaged and the car began to rise, I heard voices. Muffled at first but they became clearer and it wasn't music.

"Isn't this just a little dangerous? What if others come too?"

"Others aren't going to come. It's too risky and too dangerous."

"I don't know. I just don't have a good feeling about this."

"You worry too much. Leave it all up to me but you need to go now. She can't know who you are."

The doors to the elevator opened and a bright white lobby glared coldly at me as I stepped out of the car. I walked towards the steel gray reception desk, glancing around to see if I could recognize the owners of the voices I heard, but there was no one else in the lobby. The older woman behind the desk glanced up at me over the top rims of her glasses.

"You must be Miss Sun. Ms. Winters is waiting for you. Her office is straight ahead."

She pointed down the glass hallway to my left and I gazed down its length. There were a few cubicles along the way but a grand frosted-glass office sat at the back, overlooking the pods.

"She's on her way."

At the secretary's announcement, the frosted walls of the office became clear and I saw a blonde-haired woman turn to look at me. She stayed seated and I found myself doubting my plan again. Taking a deep breath, I began to march down the hallway towards my fake-but-real boss. They had seen me; I was on their cameras everywhere. There was no turning back.

She stood when I made it to the open doorway and she waved me in.

"Miss Sun, please come in and have a seat. I hope you didn't have any issues checking in this morning."

"No ma'am," I lied, not wanting to get the constable into trouble.

"Good. Do you have your papers to give to me?"

My heart sped up again. "Um..."

She shook her head in frustration. "Just be sure to bring it tomorrow. Have a seat."

She watched me like a hawk as we both took our seats. She was an attractive woman for her age; probably closer to my father's age than my mothers. She had long, blonde hair with streaks of gray in it that highlighted the tight bun it was twisted into. Her eyes were a deep blue and there were no laugh lines around them. They reminded me of a predator's eyes. Watchful and scrutinizing. I would definitely need to be careful around her.

"Is the house working well for you? I tried to get one as close to the office as possible as I'll need you here on the spur of the moment and at odd hours of the day and night," she hesitated. "Is that a problem, Miss Sun?"

I tried to get my racing brain under control. I was expecting a nine to five job allowing my nights and evenings to find Brice. Now what was I going to do? I swallowed and nodded. "No problem at all."

She nodded her head, no emotion reflecting off of her face. "Good. We have families and children coming in at all hours. Being a social representative for the CSS means you need to be available when a child comes in."

"I didn't realize that many families came in during off hours."

"It's actually quite common so please don't make any plans during the week. When you become more experienced, I'll expect you here on the weekend shifts too but I don't work weekends so you are off the hook with that shift…for now." She stood up and smoothed out her gray dress suit. "Come along. I'll give you a tour of the facilities."

I stood up and followed her out the door. I noticed several curious heads pop up over the cubicles to get a look at me but when they saw their boss, they quickly disappeared behind their walls.

Bernadette was taller than I had expected. She had to have been close to six foot and while she wasn't thin, she wasn't heavy either. Solid was the only word that came to mind. In hand to hand combat, she would definitely be a challenge. I prayed I never had to face her like that.

She stopped at another glass office, though this one wasn't as grand as hers. "This is my COCA and my second in charge, Aurysia Winters. If I'm not here, she's the boss and can direct you in any way needed."

I jolted as I gazed at the young woman seated at her large, wooden desk. She had to have been the same age as me. She had long blonde hair and if her last name hadn't given away her relationship with Bernadette, her hair and facial features would have. She was definitely related to Ms. Winters. But the thing that fascinated me the most was her lavender eyes. They weren't exactly the same color as mine; they were deeper and darker. I had never met anyone else who had them.

"It's nice to meet you," I smiled, hoping I found a somewhat friendly face. I was wrong.

"Did you explain the schedule and that while she's not obligated to work weekends right now, she will be in the near future?"

Bernadette smiled slightly. "Yes, I did. You will have another warm body here on the weekends soon."

"Good." She turned her cold eyes on me. "Ms. Winters will give you the tour of our facility. I expect you to have the layout memorized. If there's an emergency in the southwest wing, I expect you to know where that is at and to be there immediately. Understood?"

I stared back at the emotionless face. "Yes. Understood."

She glanced back down at the computer screen in her desk, obviously dismissing me.

Ms. Winters left the office and continued down the hall to locked double doors. "We don't horse around or socialize here. This is a work place and we all take our jobs very seriously. Lives are on the line and nothing can be missed. Do you understand?"

I was getting tired of people asking me if I understood or not. I wasn't an idiot and was beginning to resent being treated as one. "I understand perfectly. I have no intention of socializing with *anyone* here."

She eyed me tersely at my short retort and I met her gaze. She was the enemy and I wouldn't forget that. She, her beliefs and all she stood for were what tore my family apart and separated me from my brother. I wouldn't underestimate her.

She pulled out her badge and held it up to the scanner. The doors clicked open and we began walking down the hall.

"These are our holding cells. We try to keep the Addictors on the left and the Payment Repudiators on the right. Just in case you weren't clear on the names, the Addictors are the ones who repeatedly are caught doing drugs or alcohol of any kind. We have a one-time offense rule. If you are caught doing drugs or alcohol, the CSS will come in and take the children while the parents fulfill a drug dependency course mandated by the Dominion. If they are caught doing them again, the children are permanently taken from the home and the parents are sterilized."

I tried to hold back the nausea that filled my gut. I had never heard of the Dominion forcibly sterilizing people. This wasn't public knowledge. I kept my mouth shut and tried to close out the screams of parents crying for their children. I glanced in another cell and a wild-haired creature was beating on the floor, screaming and laughing. Their face was so distorted and bloody that I couldn't tell if it was male or female.

"We often get the Addictors who despite being sterilized and losing their children, still dabble in synthetic drugs. Unfortunately, this one created a bad batch and it scrambled her brains. She's been clean for over three months but her mind never recovered. She often thinks there are things crawling everywhere, including her face. We were going to euthanize her but she's a great example of why citizens shouldn't dabble with drugs. If she's still around in six months, we will try some new drug therapy on her that our scientists are experimenting with now. If that fails, she will be eliminated."

I looked over at Bernadette to see if she was joking. The sour look on her face told me she wasn't. "She's not an animal to be put on display and experimented on. What happened to compassion to fellow human beings? This is someone's daughter, someone's mother."

Bernadette sniffed down her nose at me, obviously disgusted. "No, this *used* to be someone's daughter and mother. Now, it's just a meat sack. *She* chose to take the drugs, to ruin her life. Now she's going to help prevent thousands of others from trying drugs. Her sacrifice will help others.

"Now if you are ready to move on from your judgmental, inexperienced comments, we will continue."

I glanced back at the woman in the cell. Her brown eyes caught mine and the fear they held also communicated acknowledgement of where she was and that she was sane, even if it was only in that moment. I felt a chill run up my back and I tried to shake it off.

"The Repudiators are held here if they get behind on their land or business payments," Bernadette continued. "They have to take a money management course and have six years of successful tax payments before their children are returned to them."

The nausea intensified. "Six years? Isn't that a long time for children to be away from their parents?"

She turned and glared at me. "Not long enough, in my opinion. Six years of irresponsible parents teaching their offspring how to become irresponsible adults." She turned her back on me and we continued down the hall. "Tax season is coming up so these rooms will be filled within the next two weeks. As you can see, Addictors are year-round so these rooms are usually filled. We try and move them out as fast as possible but we are short on sterilization doctors."

"How do they get the drugs and alcohol if it's illegal and not sold anywhere?"

"You're a little naive to the ways of society, Miss Sun. That's surprising. Hoodlums and lawbreakers still find ways to make their drugs and alcohol from various means. We can't stop them from buying cleaning products in the stores, or fruits and grains from the farmers. Until we can go to a completely IV infused meal schedule, we will always be dealing with this type of degenerate behavior."

I stopped suddenly. "IV infused meals?"

She stopped and faced me, a twisted smile on her face. "Yes. It's a brilliant idea and one the Dominion is working on implementing. Each morning when a man, woman or child checks into work or school, they will hook up to an IV and receive their daily amount of sustenance. It will contain all of the vitamins and minerals a body needs, other than water. This will eliminate the need for grocery stores, traditional restaurants, lunch breaks…the positives are endless." She glanced to her left as a red-eyed woman pounded on the glass window of the door, screaming to be let out. "It should help eliminate the depraved who corrupt our society and way of life."

"But won't there be complications with being stuck by needles every day?" My mind was racing at the horrific image of families no longer having meals around the table. The smell of supper as a mom or dad were busy making meals. Of becoming machines for no other use than to produce income for a fascist society.

"No. Not at all. Our brilliant scientists are working on having a permanent port installed into the arm. This will allow easy access for blood draws, injections and sustenance. Granted, it might be slightly painful at first but once we get the adult and young adult population equipped, we can then focus on the infants as soon as they are born. They will be ported right after birth and won't remember a thing."

"That sounds horrific," I whispered, unable to hold back my revulsion.

"It's not horrific. It's progress and advancement in society," she glared at me. "It's creating a better society for a productive and clean population. No more diseases, no more drug addictions, no more law breakers."

I could tell I had made her mad and I didn't want to create any doubt as to my work ethics. "I can see now, why you would be excited about it. A better civilization would be wonderful." I smiled and hoped she believed me.

She continued to stare at me; trying to decide if I was lying to her or not. She finally nodded and continued down the hallway. "Yes, it would be wonderful."

We reached the end of the hallway to another set of double doors. She scanned her badge and walked through. "Here we have the holding cells for the rule breakers. They are the ones who know better but decide to go against Dominion policy anyway."

I glanced at the people behind the glass doors. Some of them were very old; older than my parents. There were bruises on their arms and legs that the short-sleeved shirts and pants didn't hide. My first guess was that these were the ones who didn't escape during the revolution. These were probably some of the original Crows. My heart ached for them and I felt the heat and the tears behind my eyes. I squeezed them shut tightly; I couldn't afford to have my cover blown now. If Bernadette saw any compassion for these people, she would throw me into a cell next to them.

I focused my thoughts on Finn and the rest of the free Crows, and of Brice. My mission here was to get him home but I already knew it wouldn't end there. I would come back and free these people. They deserved to be saved and not forgotten behind the iron walls.

My determination and plans for the future bolstered me and I straightened, following Bernadette down the corridor. We turned the corner and a large glass room loomed in front of us. It appeared to be a dental operating room with a reclining dental type chair and various trays around it. Long, delicate robotic arms dangled from the ceiling next to the chair.

I couldn't help my gasp as I stared at the body in the chair. Brice. It was all I could do to stop myself from launching myself at Bernadette and grabbing her badge to unlock the glass door and free my brother. I felt a tear slip down my face and I couldn't stop it. He was almost unrecognizable.

His jaw on the left side was a gaping hole of meat and bone. It looked like they had detonated his PIM. His eye on that side was swollen shut, rainbow colors of red, purple and yellow bruising surrounded the area. His arms were strapped down to the chair, as were his ankles but his form was limp.

"If you are going to be in this position, Miss Sun, I suggest you gain a stronger demeanor. You will see a lot of things that are worse than this. You have to remember that it's for the greater good of the Dominion."

I hadn't realized she was watching me and I angrily swiped the tears away. "Yes ma'am. I guess I just wasn't expecting all of the blood and gore."

"Well get used to it. There are many times we need to detonate PIM's or we need to extract information. This is a defector. One of the rebels who call themselves Crows. Our top Collectivism Socialist's constabulary caught him during a raid a few weeks back. We are now extracting any information about them from him. Once we are done with the extraction, he will be eliminated."

I could feel her scrutinizing me but I refused to meet her stare. I focused on Brice and everything I was going to do to the Dominion once I got him home safe. "Have you been able to extract anything?"

She didn't say anything, taking a long moment before turning her gaze towards Brice and answering me. "No. Unfortunately they had compromised the programming of his PIM and it had to be destroyed. We couldn't risk them gaining access to our computer banks if they had a reverse tap on it. He's set for termination at the end of the week."

"Wouldn't it make more sense to use these criminals for experimentation of the ports? Not only would regular citizens be spared from potential mistakes but you could also have the living hosts for future experiments."

"Very clever and creative, Miss Sun. My daughter, Aurysia, has suggested this and it's been implemented already but I applaud your outside thinking."

I met her eyes, keeping mine impersonal. "Thank you, Ms. Winters. I hope to learn a lot from you and your daughter."

"Yes, I hope you do too," she glanced at her watch and turned back towards the way we came. "I'm due in for a meeting so I'll be leaving you with Aurysia for the rest of the tour and day. Lunch is at noon and you have twenty minutes. I'm sure she will go over all of that information with you.

"I expect to see you here at nine a.m. sharp tomorrow morning."

I turned towards her and stuck out my hand to shake hers. "Thank you for all of your guidance this morning, Ms. Winters. I'll be here promptly at nine."

She glanced down at my extended hand and pursed her lips. With a frown, she tucked both of her hands behind her back and gave me a cold smile. "Yes, well, then nine is when you and I will continue your training. Until then."

She turned to the left as the doors opened and I continued down the hallway towards Aurysia's office. I wasn't sure why she didn't shake my hand. As far as I knew, there hadn't been an outbreak of any viruses or diseases lately.

Aurysia's door was still open and she was busy reading something on her computer, her head down and a slip of blonde hair hanging over her ear and resting on the desk. I knocked lightly, not wanting to startle her.

"Come in, Miss Sun," she sighed irritatingly. "Daylight is wasting and we have a lot to cover."

I frowned for a second before I caught myself as I moved towards the guest chair. I didn't understand why she held such obvious hostility towards me. Maybe she didn't have enough coffee this morning or she was late to work. After meeting her mother, I didn't see Bernadette being any easier on her own daughter than she was with her other employees.

I sat down and folded my hands in my lap and waited. She didn't glance up or even acknowledge me as she typed and swiped on the glass computer screen in her desk. When five minutes passed, she finally looked up at me, her lavender eyes meeting my own.

"I'll be taking you to meet up with your constable. He will be your shadow and protector. If any civilians get out of hand, they are the ones who are your shield.

"You will not go anywhere without one of them. Do you understand?"

I swallowed, my mind racing. How was I supposed to explore the holding facility to see how to get Brice free if a constabulary was always with me? I nodded, hoping that one of my brilliant ideas would pop into my head before Friday.

She stood as she grabbed her badge from the corner of the desk. "If you have any questions or concerns that your constable can't answer, you will come to me. If I can't help you, only then do you go to Ms. Winters. Is that clear?"

"Crystal." I hated the rude way she was talking to me; like I was a child. She wasn't any older than me.

She stood in front of me, her glittering eyes not holding back the contempt she obviously felt for me. "If you have a problem with CSS rules, I will happily contact headquarters and have you located to a facility that suits you better."

I could feel the blood seeping from my face. If they relocated me, I'd never have a chance to get Brice out. I shook my head and dropped my eyes. "No, ma'am. I don't have any problems with the rules."

I didn't raise my eyes to hers again, waiting for her as she stood judging me. I hated every second and it felt like an eternity but finally I heard her grunt and she stepped towards the door.

"Good. I don't need any problem interns."

We walked past the double doors that led to the holding cells and entered the third set of doors. She scanned her badge as her mother had just thirty minutes earlier and we entered a long, gray hallway. There were no windows in between the double doors at either end, nor were there any pictures or paintings. Typical Dominion décor; gray and blank.

My mom once told me that there used to be large, grand museums that held colorful paintings created by various artists. She and my dad used to go them when they were dating because she loved them so much.

They were destroyed after the Dominion took over. Imagination was dangerous, they said, so all forms of it were destroyed and banned. No more paintings, or books, other than the books they used to teach the basics of education. She missed them so much that I think that was the reason she took photographs of the things she loved and hung them in our home. She wanted to keep the memory alive of beautiful and inspiring objects in her house. Like her own mini museum.

The electrical hum of the second double doors opening brought me back from my musings. We stepped into a large room with several cubicles. Constables in uniform milled about. Several of them were talking over by the coffee pot but when they looked up and saw who had walked in, they scattered and went their separate ways. Aurysia must be a usurper in her own right.

She ignored them and marched over to a large cubicle in the corner. A tall, mountain of a man rose and I felt all of the blood rush from my face and my sight became spotted and blurry. My heart began to pound and I felt faint. Standing before me was the soldier in my vision. His blonde hair and icy blue eyes didn't hold any warmth as they bore into mine. I was frozen to the spot, unable to tear my eyes from his.

"So this is the ant I'm supposed to show around?"

His voice was just as cold as I remembered and I couldn't stop my shudder.

Aurysia turned and looked at me as if I was something disgusting stuck to the bottom of her shoe. "This is Miss *Sun*. She's the new intern," she turned and looked at the Mountain before looking at me again. "Miss Sun, this is Derek. You will stick to him like glue, understood?"

I tore my eyes away from him and nodded, unable

to formulate any words. I was trying desperately to slow my beating heart and convince my mind not to engage my body's flight mechanism. Everything screamed in my head to get out.

"We will be just fine, Miss Winters," his tone softened when he talked to her. "Won't we, Miss Sun?"

I swallowed, pushing the constricting lump down my throat and nodded. I couldn't meet his eyes. "Yes," I choked. "No problems."

The corner of Aurysia's mouth tugged into a smile and she walked away, leaving us alone.

"So Miss Sun, tell me what got you into CSS work?"

"I enjoy working with people." The lie slid off my tongue smoothly and I was proud of myself for not stuttering or vomiting on the mountain of man before me.

"You won't feel the same once you've finished out the week." He picked up the gun sitting on his desk and secured it in the holster on his hip. "Let's go."

He pushed past me and I followed along. I needed to get a grip on myself and focus on the end game. Brice.

Exiting the building, we walked over to a smaller version of an ACV. He climbed into the driver's seat as I slid in next to him.

"We are going over to an Addictor's house. A tipster turned them in for child endangerment and we need to investigate." He glanced over at me. "You are there to observe *only,* do you understand? I have been doing this a very long time and know what I'm doing."

I nodded. "Yes, I understand."

He grunted and started the engine. We drove to a neighborhood across the Dominion compound that I had never been to. I was surprised to see the homes were larger and not quite as uniform. There were different yard landscapes and the homes actually had some color.

We pulled up into the driveway of a large, two-story home. He turned the engine off and called in on his radio. "We are at the suspects home and beginning our entrance for investigation."

We began walking up the sidewalk when the large doors opened. A well-dressed man came walking out, a smile on his face. "Derek! So good to see you again. What brings you to the neighborhood?"

"Step inside, sir," Derek's voice was cold and held no hint of recognition of the man. "We have been alerted to your drug use and I'm here to investigate."

The smile dropped from the man's face. "Drug use? You know how we feel about drugs. We are on the task force to eliminate them. Derek, I demand to know what this is really about."

"Step inside sir, before I have to use force."

Derek pushed the man inside roughly. I followed behind, unsure of what to do.

"Have a seat, sir. I need to take a blood sample."

The man attempted to stand, sputtering. "You will do no such thing!"

Derek roughly shoved him back down and loomed over him. "You will comply or I will take you in for resistant behavior."

The man stilled, his face slack with fear.

"That's better," Derek leered. He pulled out a small, oval machine and grabbed the man's forearm. Jabbing it into the soft flesh, he waited for the machine to complete its scan. A red light flashed and the man began shaking his head.

"That's wrong! It's rigged or broken. We don't *take* drugs!" He turned his pleading gaze at me, acknowledging my presence for the first time. "It's a mistake, I'm telling you! This is because I'm opposed to the IV infused meal procedure, isn't it?" He looked down at the smooth, tile floor. "That bitch, Bernadette. She knew it wouldn't pass without majority votes." He looked back up at Derek. "Can't you see what this is really about? It's sneaky politics. Bernadette just wants her plan to pass but I'm standing in the way. This is her way of clearing her path. It's wrong, Derek. You and I both know it."

"Jack Higgins, you are being taken into CSS custody for positive testing for an illegal drug in your system. You wife and your children will also be taken in for testing and if all are tested positive, will be imprisoned. The children will become wards of the Dominion, their future secured with how the Dominion Collectivist Socialism feels fit. Do you understand?"

"Jack? Who's down there?"

An elegant woman who I assumed was Jack's wife, flowed gracefully down the stairs, her blue pantsuit billowing with each step.

Her eyes showed alarm at the sight before her. "Derek. What is all of this? I demand to know."

Derek turned towards the woman. "Mrs. Higgins, your husband has tested positive for illegal substances in his system. As Dominion law regulates, we now have the right to test the rest of the family. We will test you, with or without your permission. Do you comply?

I watched as her elegant face twisted with defiance. "Yes, you have my permission. You know perfectly well that I'm allergic to any synthetic substances so you won't find any in my system." She walked towards Derek with her arm held out, her palm up in forfeit.

Jack started to stand. "Sally, don't! It's a set up. The machine said I tested positive."

Derek pushed Jack back down into his seat and moved towards Sally.

I saw the doubt in her eyes as her husband's words broke through her indignation. She started to pull her arm back but Derek snatched it and shoved the machine into her soft flesh.

The machine flashed red and her eyes went wide with shock. "That's impossible! I'm allergic! I'd be dead if there were any drugs in my system."

Derek put his machine away and engaged the phone on his wrist. "Mr. and Mrs. Jack Higgins have both tested positive for illegal drugs in their system. We will be detaining both adults and searching the house for the children. We will need back up to escort the children to the Neonate Asylum."

He touched the small bulge near his jaw as he listened for the response from the CSS. Nodding his head, he pulled out a small, square box and turned towards the couple. "I am now going to restrain you. If you resist at all, I am ordered to eliminate. Do you understand?"

Both of the adults nodded, dazed looks on their faces. Derek stepped behind Sally and pulled her hands behind her back. He pushed the button on the box and a yellow electrical emission encircled both of her wrists. He did the same to Jack before he had them sit on the couch.

"You will remain here until we have searched the premises. If you try to leave, the voltaic cuffs with discharge and blow off both of your hands. Do you understand?"

They both nodded in acknowledgement and Derek moved towards the staircase that Sally had moments ago descended. I followed wordlessly. I believed Sally. The expression on her face had been one of such of disbelief that I didn't think it could be faked.

We reached the top landing and walked down the long hallway. There were several closed doors both on the right and the left. Derek looked at me and placed a finger to his lips to silence any sounds I might make. Alarm filled my gut. What the hell was he thinking; to scare these poor kids to death? If they had heard any of the yelling they were probably already scared out of their wits. I couldn't allow Derek to make it worse. I cleared my throat at which he glared at me. I was still intimidated by him but my concern for the children was greater.

"Hey guys, I'm Wi," I caught myself quickly. "Suzie. I'm here with a constable and we needed to talk to you for a moment. Can you come on out and we will go talk with your Mom and Dad?" I opened the first closed door and found a young girl, maybe ten years old sitting on her bed, her eyes as large as saucers and tears streaming down her face. I walked softly over to her and sat down on the bed next to her. Gently taking her hand in both of mine, I smiled down at her.

"It's going to be okay. We just need to make sure you aren't here in the house by yourself."

Her breath hitched and her bottom lip trembled. "Are you going to take us away from my Mommy and Daddy?"

I opened my mouth to soothe her but realized it would be a lie. I hated the Dominion more than ever in that moment. They were once again tearing families apart. "Sweetheart, your Mommy and Daddy *might* have done something wrong. They need to go with Mr. Derek here. He's the constable I was telling you about."

She glanced at Derek; a slight smile flickered on her face. "I know Mr. Derek. He's come here to the house sometimes. He works with Daddy."

I glanced up at Derek. His face was stone cold,

and I wondered if he had a beating heart behind his body armor. By the look on his face, I guessed not.

"That's right. He does. He is going to take your Mommy and Daddy down to CSS and talk with them there and you are going to stay with me until we can get you somewhere safe. Do you have a brother or sister with you or in the house?"

She nodded her head and wiped her nose with the back of her arm. "My little brother is in his room across the hall."

I patted her hand and stood up. "I'm going to go get him and bring him here. Then we can all play a game until another SUV gets here, okay?"

I glared at Derek as I pushed by him, ignoring his glowering. I knocked softly on the door before opening, finding the room empty. I glanced under the bed and found it empty. I checked the closet hoping to find him there, but it was also empty. I spotted a large, white toybox in the corner of the room and moved towards it. Opening the lid, I found him huddled underneath plush toy animals. He had his eyes squeezed tightly shut.

"Hey there little man. My name is Suzie. It's okay. No one is going to hurt you." I prayed that I wasn't lying. "Your sister is on her bed talking to Derek. You remember Derek, don't you?"

At the mention of Derek's name, the little boy opened his eyes and stared at me. He began to nod his head and I gently pulled the stuffed animals from the box to free him from their cocoon.

I was rapidly trying to piece everything together. I had never seen neighborhoods with such extravagant homes. These plush toys weren't available in the neighborhood I grew up in. Toys that weren't secretly made by family weren't available to us either. These were soft and made of materials that I had never felt before. Were the higher ups in the Dominion Collective Socialism allowed more privileges? It appeared so, but with those privileges obviously came with risks. I thought of Jack and Sally downstairs. He mentioned something about opposing Bernadette's IV infused meals. I wasn't sure who was higher on the Dominion ladder; Jack or Bernadette, but it was obvious today who was more powerful, or devious. Bernadette obviously won this battle. There was no denying that the machine tested both Jack and Sally positive for synthetic drugs. I saw it with my own eyes, but I have no doubt that the machine had been tampered with prior to coming to their house. I just had no way of proving it. It was a battle I had to let go. I couldn't risk Bernadette's wrath and being sent away; Brice's life depended on it.

The little boy was free of his animal swaddle and grabbed my hand for balance as he climbed out of the box. He was so small, and my heart ached at the thought that he would never be with his mom or dad again. I blinked back tears so he wouldn't become alarmed. "What's your name?"

He held onto one of my hands as we both stood. "My name is Jack Jr. and I'm six years old." He beamed up at me.

"Wow! You are so big for six!"

He nodded his head excitedly as we walked towards his sister's room. "Yep, like a giant. Mommy told me so."

"Well, Mommies aren't usually wrong." I thought of my own and my heart clenched. So many times, I'd had wished I had more time with her, but this situation made me appreciate the time that I did have with her. I should have talked with her more.

"I hear Inka!" He let go of my hand and ran into the room, climbing onto the bed next to his sister. They hugged as Derek blocked my entry with his arm across the doorway.

"What the hell do you think you're doing, Vrana?"

I wasn't sure what a vrana was, but I was sure it was an insult. "I'm trying to calm some scared little kids who are never going to see their parents again," I hissed.

I shoved his arm from the doorway and knelt down before them, placing my hands on their legs. "Derek is going with your parents and he is going to call for a car for us to take, okay? So, go ahead and get dressed and let's brush your hair, Inka. Okay?"

Both little bodies jumped off the bed and began to get ready. I glanced over to the doorway but found Derek had already left. I hoped that I would be able to stay with the kids for the rest of the day and I wouldn't have to spend any more time with him.

By the time we came down the stairs, Derek, Sally and Jack were gone. I breathed a sigh of relief having envisioned sobbing and tearful departures.

I heard an engine in the driveway and walked towards the door. I assumed it was the second CSS vehicle to come take the children and I to the Neonate asylum. The door handle twisted in my hand and I was shoved back as it was pushed open forcibly.

"What in the world do you think you are doing?"

I met Aurysia's furious eyes with my own as I caught my stumble. "I'm trying to make a really bad and scary situation better. Isn't that what the CSS is *supposed* to do? Be there for the kids?" I had quoted one of the Dominion commercials that boasted of compassion and caring for children under the Dominion care. The commercials were far from reality it seemed.

She hesitated, obviously realizing I was calling her out. I was done being the submissive, soft-spoken joke of the CSS. The previous six hours showed me I was just a warm body to fill a position. They wanted to break and twist me into their mold, and I wasn't going to do it.

She looked over my shoulder and saw the owl-eyed little moppets sitting on the couch, watching us closely.

"Yes, well, since you are new, I'll forget it this time but there are protocols we need to follow. I expect you to learn them if you want to do this job properly." She glared at me again. "Load them into the vehicle and we will go down to Neonate."

Inka jumped up and shook her head. "I don't wanna go to Neonate. Mommy said it's a bad place and that I would never have to go there."

I turned and knelt down in front of Inka. How was I going to lie my way out of this one? They trusted me and I was going to have to betray them. "Inka, I don't think it's a bad place and I'll be with you. Maybe we will see your parents there."

She stared at me with those big brown eyes and my heart clenched and twisted within my chest. "Can I bring Hoppy?"

I tried to figure out who Hoppy was, but Jack Jr.

quickly cleared up the mystery. "If she gets to bring Hoppy then I get to bring my stuffed horsey."

I patted Inka on the shoulder. "Okay but you both have to make it fast. Who can be the first back down here?"

They both raced up the stairs trying to best the other. They reminded me so much of myself and Brice that I felt the moisture well up in my eyes. I missed the simple days. Preparing for years to escape the Dominion was so much easier than what this was that I was attempting to do. But I had to save my brother from the Dominion clutches.

"You've broken so many rules, Suzie. Don't think Bernadette is going to let you off the hook so easy."

I turned to study Aurysia who was leaning against the open-door jamb, her arms crossed defiantly.

"I don't care. These kids haven't done anything wrong. They shouldn't be punished for the sins of their parents, *if* their parents truly are guilty."

Her face twisted in a frown. "What do you mean *if?* You were standing right there. You saw the tester go red, which is positive for drugs."

I took a step towards her and cocked my head curiously. "How did you know I was standing right there?"

I saw her turn red and a moment of hesitation. "I

know because it's standard protocol. Testing has to be done with a witness."

She was lying and my suspicions were firming up. They had set up Jack and Sally. "Well this *witness* believes the tester was malfunctioning. I think it needs to be inspected before I'll believe that they both tested positive."

She started to shake her head but caught herself. Her face cleared and she raised the corner of her mouth into a sneer. "That's fine. We can do that." She lifted her arm and called out over the CSS system. "Derek, Miss Sun believes that the synthetic drug testing machine is malfunctioning. Once you get to headquarters, please take it directly to ITT and have it inspected. Report back to myself and Ms. Winters as soon as you have the results." She smiled smugly at me. "Satisfied?"

My stomach and heart dropped. Derek had plenty of opportunity to exchange out the tampered SDTM. The crew at ITT would test the machine and declare it operational and Jack and Sally would be put away for who knows how long. I should've kept my mouth shut until I figured out how to get a hold of that machine.

Inka and Jack Jr. came racing down the stairs at that moment, both clutching their toys tightly in their arms. I pasted on a smile. "Easy there, racers. Looks like we have a tie! Are you ready for a ride?"

They both nodded and ran towards the car, Aurysia stood back and watched them climb into the car. I walked past her without looking at her and climbed into the back with the kids. She got into the passenger side front and ordered the driver to take us to Neonate.

I wished the ride could take longer than the twenty minutes it did. I didn't want to leave them there, scared and alone with strangers but I was powerless to do otherwise. I walked them to the doors and a CSS worker came and gathered the two of them up. Inka ran over and hugged my leg before grabbing her brother's hand and they both walked inside the brick building. It looked like they were walking into the gaping mouth of a monster and I had a moment of panic in which I wanted to scream for them to stop and snatch them out of the monster's clutches. I didn't though and within a second, they disappeared into the darkness.

I turned and climbed back into the vehicle. It was almost four o'clock. I had missed lunch, but my stomach didn't grumble. It seemed numb from all of the emotions I had experienced throughout the day. The thought of food actually made me nauseous.

We pulled into the main CSS headquarters and I quietly followed Aurysia into the building. I felt beaten and exhausted. Walking down the long, windowless corridor towards the offices, I heard arguing.

"Why didn't you *tell* me she was here? I told you she would come back for her brother."

"Stay out of it, Bradlee. This no longer has anything to do with you. We've got this under control."

"You think you do but I know her better. She has gifts, talents that you wouldn't even expect. You need to reconsider keeping her safe. Think about what an incredible asset she would be for the Dominion. The perfect, unsuspecting spy. She might even be hearing us now. Where did you say she was?"

"Her and Aurysia are taking the little brats over to Neonate. They should be back soon."

"Exactly. She could be listening to us now."

"Relax, little brother. She's not listening to us and she's not staying here...alive, but you do need to leave. If she sees you, she's going to know that we know who she is."

"Are you going to come through the doors, Miss Sun, or do you need a written invitation?"

I started, realizing Aurysia was holding one of the automatic doors open to allow me through. I jumped through the doorway, dazed. They knew who I was.

Had they always known? How was I going to get Brice out of here and both of us to safety? If they knew who I was, they would be watching me like a hawk. Panic welled up in my body and I couldn't stop shaking.

Aurysia stared at me like I was an alien. "What is wrong with you? Are you having a seizure or something?"

"I don't feel well." It wasn't a lie. I felt like I was going to vomit all over their white-tiled floor.

"Someone grab her a trashcan!" I heard Aurysia screech before the contents of my stomach blew all over the smooth floor. Because I had missed lunch, there wasn't much but it was enough to splatter over her shoes.

"Oh my god. What is wrong with you?" She stepped back and kicked off her shoes next to the wall. "Go sit out on the chairs in the waiting room and I'll have a car take you home." She glared at a woman in her cubicle staring at her. "Don't just stand there gawking, call maintenance and have this mess cleaned up. And throw away those shoes. I'll never wear them again."

I made my way out to the lobby area and sat down in one of the hard, plastic chairs. Placing my head in my hands, I cradled it there, my elbows digging into the tops of my thighs. I closed my eyes and tried to figure out the mess I was in. How was I going to get Brice out? How was I going to even get myself out? And why were they playing along with my ruse? They obviously knew why I came back.

I groaned loudly. Bradlee. I never even thought about him possibly being in the same building as I.

I jerked up as a metal trashcan appeared below me. A janitor stood back and stared at me like I was a bomb about to go off.

"If you get sick again, try and aim for the trashcan, okay?"

"Yes, sir."

He walked away in the direction I had just come. I felt guilty I had created the mess he was about to clean up. I wish he could help me with the bigger one.

I bolted upright, an idea developing underneath the fear. Maybe it was one out of desperation, but I was either going to be leaving the Dominion compound with my brother or I would die here.

I picked up the trashcan and began to stumble towards the janitor who was in fact, cleaning up my mess. I took a shaky breath, I really needed to convince this man that I was about to be sick again. "Sir…I think I dropped my pen over here…"

He shook his head. "Miss, the CSS can get you a

new pen. If you dropped it over here, you aren't going to want it back."

"Yes, but it was clipped onto my tiny notepad. I had to take notes today because we went over *so* much information and I don't want Ms. or Miss Winters to get angry with me tomorrow."

His expression softened with sympathy. "I will keep an eye out..."

I was close enough now that I pretended to slip and vomit at the same time. As he reached out to keep me from falling, I shifted my weight into him, throwing us both off balance and we went down into the wet, sloppy ruminate on the floor.

Several CSS employees ran over to help but stopped when the smell hit their noses. The janitor untangled himself from me and carefully stood before reaching down and pulling me to my feet.

"I'm so very sorry," I apologized.

He softened when he saw the sincerity in my eyes and shook his head. "It's alright, Miss. The good Lord gave us the skin He did so we can wash off the gunk after a hard day's work." He picked up his mop and nodded his head towards the exit sign. "You better get out of here before Miss *or* Ms. Winters comes back. Go home and get some rest so you are fresh tomorrow."

"But Aurysia is sending a car around to take me home."

"I'll tell them you couldn't wait and felt well enough to drive home."

I nodded and started towards the exit. "Thank you, sir. And again, I'm so sorry."

I held my breath as I slipped through the door, waiting for an alarm to go off or someone to stop me before I reached my SUV. Walking quickly, I opened the door but didn't climb in. I didn't want it smelling like my own throw up. I couldn't strip down to my underwear, but I could take off the jacket. That wouldn't help my butt. Searching the back seat, I found an emergency blanket tucked underneath. If this wasn't an emergency, I didn't know what was.

Unfolding it, I draped it over my seat, covering the cloth. I slid onto the crinkling material and started the engine. The sooner I could get back to my temporary home, the better.

SIX

AFTER TAKING THE LONGEST SHOWER in history and washing all of the day down the drain, I put my soiled clothes into the washing machine. As I picked up my jacket, I pulled the notepad and pen out of the inner pocket, along with the janitor's badge.

I felt horrible that I stole from him, but this was the only way I could see getting back into the building without being stopped. The back parking lot where the employees were just had a scanning device. I should be able to get in from there and make my way back towards Brice's holding cell.

I started the washer and went to the bedroom to sit down on the bed. I knew I needed to have a plan but other than getting in the door, I had no idea how I could get us out when we were surrounded with constabulary. Why did I think I could do this without any help from the Crows; without Finn? I closed my eyes and let the tears slip down my cheeks.

"It's because your inner soul knows exactly who you are. You come from a long line of warriors, Will."

I jerked my head up, my heart pounding as I stared into the beautiful blue eyes of my mother. "Mom..."

"You have gifts, Willow. You've only experienced a few of them but as the pressure begins to build to save your brother, trust in those gifts. You can also use them to call upon the Crows to help."

I shook my head, "They can't help me, I have no way of letting them know I'm in trouble." I angrily wiped a tear from my cheek. "Besides, they don't see me as a Crow. Just a silly girl who keeps causing problems like going off into Dominion territory without any plans or backup. I'll never be one of them."

"No, you won't, Willow, because you're not a Crow. Your heritage is grander than that. You come from a long line of women whose talents are not only in combat but the ability to manipulate and read the minds of others," she smiled softly. "Your grandmother compared us to the Gyrfalcon because like them, we are fierce predators and can change our appearance to suit our environment."

"If she compared us to these falcons, why did she name our faction the Crows?"

"Because the faction doesn't have the same talents and abilities as we do, but crows are still intelligent and brave predators. They are cunning and have the ability to adapt and overcome change."

"Why didn't you tell me any of this while you were still alive?" I didn't wipe the tears that were now streaming down my face. I missed seeing my mother every day, I missed her hugs, but mostly I missed these talks with her.

She moved as if to hold my hand but stopped, both of us knowing she wasn't able to. "There are things that have happened that you don't know about yet. Things that I'm still not able to share with you. When the time is right, the truth will be exposed. Until then, know that I love you, always and forever."

"Don't go yet, Mom. I still need you. I miss you and I'm scared."

Her form vanished into a wisp and was gone. I felt a mixture of emotions twist in my gut, wanting her back so badly. Anger and pain; two of my faithful companions since her murder swirled like a tornado in my soul. I focused on the spot where she had sat and tried to conjure her back.

Bluish tendrils of smoke formed and began to dance before me. I focused harder on my mother's face and it emerged before my eyes. "Mom!"

She began to laugh and kissed something in front of her that wasn't me. "Kennet, they are still kids. Brothers and sisters do this. It's called playing. Let them play and if one happens to get hurt, we will just bury them in the backyard."

I realized this was the conversation she and Dad had had the day my PIM malfunctioned, and I was detained. It seemed so long ago. I reached out to see if I could touch her form but like a specter, the minute my hand touched any area of her form, it spun and churned. When I removed my hand, her image appeared solid once more.

My mind began to race as I remembered the constabulary soldiers I had seen with Finn. They hadn't been solid like Mom, they had stayed the translucent, blue ghosts and I wondered if it was because I hadn't been there to see it first-hand like I had with Mom. It was something I wanted to find out.

I bent my head and closed my eyes, focusing on the face I wanted to see so badly. I imagined the scar that ran from his left eye and continued on a path towards his ear. I focused on his warm breath on my lips when I thought we were going to kiss. I focused on the feeling of being in his arms during my first dance.

"Willow?"

I looked up and saw him standing before me. "Finn?"

"Am I dreaming? Is that really you, Willow?"

I started to giggle. "Yes, Finn. It's me. I guess this is one of my gifts that Mom was telling me about."

"How are you? Are you safe? Have you seen Brice?"

"I'm safe but Finn, they know who I am. I heard Bradlee talking with Derek."

"Who's Derek?"

"Remember the huge constable I was telling you about in my vision? His name is Derek and he's Bradlee's older brother. I think he and Aurysia have a thing for each other but I'm not sure..." I wandered off in thought as I tried to recount everything that had happened that day.

"Who's Aurysia?"

I jerked back to the present. "She's the daughter of Bernadette Winters. She also has lavender eyes, which I thought was so cool but she's as cold and ruthless as her mom. She's second in command at the CSS and I get the strong impression she doesn't like me."

"If she knows who you are then she won't. You need to come back, Willow. If they know who you are, they'll be watching."

"I can't, Finn. I saw Brice. He's alive but only for a few more days. He looks horrible. They detonated his PIM," my voice hitched.

"I can have a group ready to leave by morning, Willow. Don't go anywhere until we get there. We will bring *both* of you home. I miss you. I don't want to lose you."

I smiled up at him. It felt so good to see his face and hear his voice. I knew he wanted to protect me but time was running out. I needed to make my move tonight.

"Thank you for my presents," I changed the subject.

"You are welcome. I didn't want you to be there unarmed."

"When you talk to Duncan, will you ask him about the Addictors and the SDTM? I think they are using it to falsely accuse innocent people of drug use."

"Why would they want to do that?"

"That's what I'm trying to figure out but from what I'm piecing together, it's one way of getting opposition eliminated to get bills passed."

"That's a dirty way of doing it."

"Yes, especially since it removes innocent children from their homes, too."

"Just don't do anything rash. Get a good night's sleep and we will be there before the lunch hour."

I shook my head. "Just wait for me at the entry road next to the highway and bring a medical team. Brice is going to need one as soon as possible."

"Willow..."

"I miss you, Finn." I cleared my head and his image disappeared. The line of communication broken. I wondered if I would be able to recall him again, but didn't try. I didn't need him to argue with me to try and change my mind. I had to make a plan and my time was running out.

SEVEN

THE BLACK PANTS AND BLOUSE blended in with the black cloak. I was surprised at how well I was able to hide in the shadows. I had left through the back door and made my way around the front of the house to avoid any neighbors seeing me. I breathed a sigh of relief when I saw there wasn't anyone out on the sidewalks.

Climbing into the SUV, I made my way back towards CSS headquarters. Pulling up to the fenced employee parking area, I took a deep breath as I held out the janitor's badge to the scan pad. Knowing that cameras were recording everything, I closed my eyes and imagine his face looking back instead of my own.

I wouldn't have any idea if it worked or not until I was either met by constables or if I was left alone. I prayed Mom was right when she said we had the ability to manipulate what others saw.

The gate buzzed and slowly opened, allowing me passage. Taking a deep breath, I pulled into a parking space and shut off the engine. I had strapped my quiver to my back and had it hidden under my cloak. If I needed it, all I had to do was throw the black and purple material over my shoulder to expose my arrows.

Walking towards the door, I calmed my nerves. I had to keep a clear head and keep in mind that to everyone in the building I was Clarence Goodman; one of the CSS janitors.

The large room that held all of the cubicles was eerily silent. Half of the lights were extinguished causing large shadows to loom ominously. I moved towards the double doors that led to the holding cells. I saw a light on in Aurysia's office and stopped. What was she still doing here? I glanced around trying to see if there was another way to the double doors but any way I chose, I would have to pass her office. I closed my eyes and took a deep breath, praying she was so engrossed in her work that she wouldn't notice me.

I walked smoothly by the glass windows, glancing

in. She was sitting at her desk, focused on the computer screen. Hopefully she wouldn't notice me at all.

"Hey! You there. What are you doing here?"

"Um…"

She waved her hand like waving away an insect. "Never mind. Did you throw my shoes away like I asked? Disgusting creature, wasn't she? And to think I have to deal with her all day tomorrow."

She was no longer looking at me nor did it appear like she was even talking to me. She continued mumbling to herself and I made my way towards the double doors. She really didn't like me. I scanned the pad and the doors swung in, allowing me passage. I stepped through and waited until they closed before walking towards the torture room where Brice had been. I saw a familiar flash of blue catching my attention.

Jack and Sally Higgins were sitting on a hard bench. Sally's mascara had smeared, creating dark raccoon smudges around her eyes, her beautifully coifed hair sticking out in disarray. Jack didn't appear any different other than being pale and resigned. I wanted to help them. I wanted to reunite them with their children. They didn't deserve this. I didn't know what their role in the Dominion was, they might not be good people. I did know that they had been set up; they were not synthetic drug users.

Jack glanced up sorrowfully and froze. His mouth twisted into an O and I realized I hadn't been keeping up my mask. I leapt forward and out of his sight. I couldn't help them now. It was Brice's turn but maybe I could see if the other Crows could help me get them out.

I slipped down the rest of the hallway without incident and stepped into the medical torture room. It was clean, no signs of Brice's blood anywhere. I hadn't seen him in any of the rooms in the hallway. Where had they taken him?

I saw a door to the left of the room. It was solid and white with another scanning pad beside the knob. I stepped up and scanned Clarence's badge. It lit up green and the latch clicked. I pushed it open and found Brice's prone body on the bed. I raced over and knelt beside him. His back was towards me and I gently placed my hand on his shoulder.

"Brice. Brice, it's me, Willow. I've come to get you out."

He rolled over to face me and I couldn't stop the gasp. The flesh and muscle by his mandible were hanging loosely, his back teeth exposed. His eyes were large and fearful, and I could see his tongue working in his mouth.

"Shhh, Brice, it's okay. I'm not here to hurt you. I'm here to take you home."

He shook his head and sat up slowly. Once upright, he kept pointing towards the door.

I couldn't stop the tears. His hands were mangled, broken and dislocated. Bruises tracked up his arms and along his neck. I could see from the neckline of his shirt that they traced down his chest too. "I'm not leaving you here. They've done enough to you. You are my brother and the only family I have left," I choked. "So, get your ass up so we can get out of this hellhole."

His face twisted and a monstrous noise came from his mouth. "Maaaaaaah."

It took me a moment before I realized what he was trying to say. I dropped my head and nodded, unable to meet his eyes. "Yes, they are both dead. Mom killed Dad when he was trying to kill me." I met his gaze. "She saved my life."

"Ssssiiiiiiisss."

"I'm here, Brice but we have to go now before they figure out who I am."

"Sssiiiiiiiisss…"

I was starting to get frustrated. I couldn't understand him, and my instincts were telling me we had to move and move *now*. "Get up now, Brice."

I helped him to his feet, his body weighing heavily on my shoulders. I had forgotten how big he really was. We stumbled towards the door, both of us gaining our bearings when I felt a shock run through my arm. My mind was screaming to turn around and hide, that we couldn't go back the way we came. I glanced around the room, trying to figure out where to go but there didn't appear to be any other doors.

I caught sight of a flash and noticed one of the body doors was slightly ajar. I shuddered, knowing that this was where they stored the dead bodies until they were disposed of but I didn't see another option. "Brice, we need to hide in the morgue refrigerators."

He shook his head, his eyes wide.

"Now is no time to be squeamish. If we don't hide, we might be in there for real."

He pushed me towards them but instead of opening up one of the doors, he pushed open a tall storage door. It was filled with towels and cotton batting. I didn't understand why he thought we could both fit in there, it was filled with supplies.

He grunted and reached up towards the left top corner and pushed. The back of the closet swung back and revealed a long passageway. I looked up at him and smiled. "Even being tortured, you still pay attention to the little things," I tried to joke but realized it fell short.

He still attempted to smile, and he gently pushed

me forward. Once I stepped through, I helped him duck down and get through the opening. We closed the door again, hoping that it wouldn't be discovered that we had slipped through.

Following the corridor, there were several areas where the passage split into other directions. I hesitated at each intersection, wondering which way to go. Since Brice had never been down this way, he wasn't sure either. I tried to pull up the exterior image of the building and choose the passages that would take us to where I parked the SUV. My instincts were still screaming at me that we weren't safe yet.

We had gone down a dimly lit corridor when I heard voices. Hiding in a darkened doorway, we stayed frozen.

"I don't understand how you could let them get away."

"It's not like I ushered her into the building and showed her where Brice was. And why weren't you watching her like you were supposed to do? Some great constable *you* are."

"I told you, she never came out of the house while I was watching. One second the SUV was there, the next it was gone. At least I had the common sense to realize she was coming back here," Derek's voice was dripping with anger.

"Oh, big leap there. Of course she was coming back for Brice. Why do you think she came back to the Dominion in the first place?"

"You sure are eager to place blame on me but aren't so ready to accept any yourself. Why weren't *you* watching her? And why don't you have any of these special gifts she seems to possess? She's *your* sister."

I sucked in my breath, trying to replace the air that had just been sucked out of my lungs. How in the hell could Aurysia be my sister?

"*Half*-sister, jerk. Why do you have to keep bringing that up?"

"Because I think it's pretty cool that she has some of these talents and I think it would be cooler if my girlfriend had some cool talents too."

"Shhh. Did you hear that?"

"No, I didn't hear anything."

"*Twenty-six-seven, we have confirmed the suspect's SUV is parked in the employee parking lot.*"

"Twenty-six-seven here. Affirmative. Do not let that SUV leave under any circumstances."

"*Romeo. Copy that.*"

"Are you happy now? They haven't left the building."

"I'll be happy when they are both in custody and I can get rid of Willow, once and for all."

"Where's the sisterly love?"

"Shut up, jerk."

I stayed frozen with my back against the wall trying to absorb the conversation I just heard. How could Aurysia be my sister? Mom never talked about having another child so it had to be Dad. But she was my age. Did he know? Did Mom or Brice? I glanced up at Brice who was staring at me patiently.

"Did you know Aurysia was my sister?"

He nodded slowly.

"Have you known for a long time?"

He shook his head. At least he hadn't kept a secret from me all of our lives.

There was too much information to process and I knew I didn't have the time now to do it. They knew where my SUV was, and we weren't going to be able to escape in it.

I turned down a hallway opposite the one I was going to take towards the employee parking lot. I wanted to run as fast as I could just to escape the CSS building, but Brice was having a hard time keeping up. If his hands were that mangled, I could only imagine what they did to his legs. We were both lucky that he could walk at all.

I turned another corner and ran into something hard. Knocking me back into Brice, I quickly regained my footing and found myself staring into familiar bright blue eyes.

"Willow, they are looking for you and Brice but I'm sure you already know that. If you want to get out of here safely, you need to trust me."

I felt Brice push towards Bradlee and I pushed back to stop him. I glared at Bradlee. "And why should I trust you? You are the reason the Crow camp was destroyed and the reason I had to come back to get Brice. You are the reason my parents are dead."

"You're wrong, Willow. Well, I mean wrong about most of it," he ran his fingers through his hair. "I was helping the Dominion and your father destroy the Crow's faction, but I wanted only to scatter the community and bring home a very important family. You have gifts, Willow. Gifts that are yet to be explored and if we could figure out how to use that DNA…"

"Oh, so you just wanted to use me as a guinea pig for experiments. Forget about any kind of life that I wanted to live."

He shook his head. "No, nothing like that. They would just need to take a sample, *one time*, from each member of your family and it would give them years of material to research."

"Well they can't do that anymore considering both of our parents are dead. And didn't you do enough harm to Brice? You honestly think I'm going to cooperate with the twisted mentality of the Dominion? I saw what your brother, Derek, did to Sally and Jack Higgins. They aren't Addictors. It was all set up to clear Bernadette's path for IV infused feeding ports."

He dropped his head and shook it. "I *knew* you were listening to us. Absolutely incredible," he looked back up at me. "Where were you when you heard Derek and I talking? Two blocks away? In the parking lot?"

"I was in the corridor coming in from the parking lot."

I saw his smile slip slightly. "Oh, but still, that's pretty incredible since we were in the constabulary area."

While he was mumbling, I slowly tried to pull my cloak back to access my bow and quiver. He glanced up and caught my movement, frowning. He waved his hand. "You don't need that, Willow. Put it away."

"I'm not going back with you willingly, Bradlee. I'll die here defending my brother before I'll ever go back to living under the Dominion rule."

"And what a waste that would be," he met my eyes and held them. "I'm not going to kill you nor am I going to let the Dominion kill you. That would be such a waste. Do you think if Aristotle met a unicorn, he would want to destroy it?"

"I'm not a unicorn, Bradlee. I'm a human being."

"But not any human being. You are as special as a unicorn, Willow. Which is why I'm going to help you escape."

He glanced over his shoulder down the corridor I was taking. "We can't go that way, though. That leads you into the heart of the CSS and near the constabulary office. You need to go back the way you came, through the holding cells and back out into the office area."

"We can't go that way. Aurysia's office is that way and they have already done something to my SUV."

"Aurysia is with Derek looking for you. And you won't be going out to the parking lot. You are going out through the front. My truck is parked along the side. Here's the fob to start it. Once you get off of CSS property drive directly to free zone territory." He looked up at Brice and I saw sorrow paint his eyes. "I'm so sorry, Brice. I never thought they would do this to you. They promised your Dad that you and your family would be treated like royalty. I believed them. I can never make it up to you for the torture you've endured and the loss of your parents, but I can do this. I'm really sorry."

I wasn't sure if this was a ruse or not but memories of us laughing and practicing hand-to-hand combat came flooding back. I had even had a crush on him when I had been frustrated with Finn. I *wanted* to trust him.

"You're going to have to trust me, Willow. I'm the only shot you have right now."

"How did you…"

"You don't have to have special gifts to see what was running through your mind," he chuckled. He brought his wrist up to his lips, engaging the two-way radio. "I saw them in lower level four. They are heading northwest."

I felt my heart start beating faster. We were in the northwest corridor.

"Relax. Level four is two levels below us but it's not going to take them long before they figure it out. Go back as fast as you can and I'll stall them."

I studied him for a second wondering if he was setting us up or not. He didn't make sense and I didn't have the time to ask why all of this had to happen this way. I guess it didn't matter at this point. I still hated him but was thankful for this opportunity to get out. "Thank you, Bradlee."

"Get out of here before I change my mind, okay?" he growled.

I turned and looked at Brice. "Can you run?"

He took a deep breath and nodded slightly, a humming noise escaping the side of his jaw.

I took of his hand and we turned back the way we came. Brice could only do a shuffling, hop-run but it was faster than I expected him to be able to go. We didn't run into any soldiers in the corridors and I was feeling hopeful. I pulled out Clarence's badge and held it up to the pad. The double doors swung open. My heart felt like it was going to leap out of my chest and I instinctively pulled out my bow and nocked an arrow. Standing at the other end was a startled constable. His eyes looked as wide as mine felt, both of us unsure of what move to make.

I felt fingers tingle the back of my neck and into my hair and the images of all of the constabulary apparitions I had seen at the destroyed Crow camp came swirling in behind us. I heard Brice grunt and the constable's eyes grow wider. They could see them too? I didn't have time to ask, I knew that this was the best distraction we were going to have.

I held my bow up and screaming like a banshee, raced towards the soldier. The phantoms followed suit, keeping up with Brice and me. The constable never had a chance to call on his watch. He raised his rifle and started firing at the most daunting soldier that was running right next to Brice. I aimed and just as I let my arrow loose, a loud clunking noise startled me. The arrow struck his shoulder instead of his heart, but nobody had time to counter. The doors to the holding cells slid open and we were suddenly surrounded by Payment Repudiators and Addictors.

Seeing all of us running towards the soldier must have been a sight because he was stumbling backwards, holding the arrow that was still sticking out from his shoulder. He hit the pad to the doors and they swung open as he stumbled back, leaving room for *all* of us to run into the cubicle and lobby area.

I turned towards the front doors, grabbing onto Brice's arm. The wraiths disappeared but the detainees didn't. They continued running through any exit doors they could. I saw Jack and Sally race towards the side door. As Jack held the door open for Sally, our eyes caught for a moment. He smiled slightly and nodded. I felt a slight smile answer his. I was glad they were escaping. I just hoped they could figure out how to be reunited with Jack Jr. and Inka.

We slid out the front doors and side-stepped to the left to stay hidden behind the large juniper bushes. I knew cameras were everywhere and they would be searching for us. I spotted Bradlee's truck and we crept towards it. I was glad it was dark and my cloak helped to keep us hidden.

Slipping behind the driver's wheel, I started the truck. Brice buckled up and I placed the truck in gear and headed down the road. I wanted to floor it and get to the border gate as soon as I could but racing down the dark streets would only draw attention to us. It was all I could do to keep our speed at the limit.

"You let her go?"

Aurysia's screeching voice startled me and the truck swerved with my jerk.

I glanced in the back seat expecting to see her. The seats were empty.

"I told you we couldn't trust your brother."

Bradlee's pleading voice, while sounding sincere, didn't hold any fear. "What was I supposed to do? She had her bow pointed right at my heart. I told you what a crack shot she was."

"But you didn't tell the rest of us, little brother. How do you think that looks?"

"He's covering for her. He *likes* her."

"Yes, I do, Aurysia. She's kind and fierce and special. All of the attributes *you* seem to lack."

"Derek! Are you going to let him talk to me like that?"

"While we are wasting time, Willow and her brother are getting away."

"No, she's not. I was expecting something like this, so I had trackers installed in her pastries that were delivered to her house."

"How can you be sure she ate the right one?"

"I had them baked in *all* of them and when she showed up here this morning, I had IT activate them. It shows one is attached to her esophagus and working properly. We will let them go and she will lead us to the camps."

"You think she knows where the Montana camp is?"

"If she doesn't know now, I'm sure she will soon. She just broke into the Dominion and saved her precious brother. She'll be a hero."

"I hope you are right, Aurysia, or your mother will punish us all."

"I'm right. We just need to be patient."

The lump that had formed in my throat was constricting and I found it difficult to breathe. I couldn't go back to camp. Not if I had a tracker in my body. I glanced over at Brice, who had his head resting against the glass, his eyes closed. I had to get him back to the Crows. They would be able to heal his body and hopefully allow him to talk again.

We started through the long tunnel that would lead us to the other side of the city. It felt like years ago that my family and I were traveling through the tunnel, holding our breath and wondering if the constabulary would be waiting for us on the other side.

This time I knew they wouldn't be. They were allowing our escape.

We exited the tunnel for a second time without any resistance. I drove up to the large, looming gate and pulled out my original travel badge. It didn't matter that it was Suzie Sun's badge. They knew who I was, but they didn't know that I was wise to their knowledge.

The gate slid open and I drove on through. As I drove along in silence, I kept glancing at Brice. He was the only family I had left and I loved him so much. My heart ached at the sight of the gaping opening on the side of his face. His jaw appeared to be dislocated at the mandible and I shuddered, relieved that the PIM's detonation hadn't decapitated him. He was alive.

I sped through the valley where my family had left our SUV, not even bothering to glance at the spot. It was no longer relevant and felt like a lifetime ago. As we climbed out of the valley, the trees began to thicken and I slowed the truck down. The turn off would be coming up and I didn't want to miss it.

I saw the road as I passed it and cursed quietly. Stopping the truck, I backed up on the lonely highway and turned the wheels onto the gravel path. We had only traveled a hundred yards when the road was blocked by a large ACV. I couldn't stop the grin that infected my face. It was *my* ACV, Bernice.

The turret swung slowly and centered on the truck. I knew it was being manned by a Crow and that they didn't know who was in the truck yet but I wasn't worried. There was no way that ACV would fire upon me. It would experience another malfunction before that happened.

I placed a hand softly on Brice's arm. "We are here, Brice. Safe with the Crows."

He looked up, his eyes wide in alarm and I heard a guttural gasp.

"It's okay. That's my ACV, Bernice." I laughed as he looked at me like I'd lost my mind. "A lot happened while you were gone. And yes, this machine appears to have a personality."

I opened the door and slowly slid out. The ACV's hatch opened and Finn popped out of the top. He quickly scrambled down and came running towards me. He scooped me up into his arms and I rested my head in his shoulder. It felt so good to be held by him and I wanted to stay there forever but I knew I couldn't. More important things had to come first.

"Finn, Brice is in bad shape. He needs medical help as soon as possible."

"We brought some EMT's like you said. They can start working on him on our way back to camp." He released me and moved towards the truck to help Brice. "We need to get back though; it'll be two o'clock in the morning before we reach camp."

"Finn…" It came out as a whisper, but he heard me and stopped, turning to face me.

"I can't go back to the camp. They are expecting it. They planted a tracking chip in me. It's in my throat."

"Once we get back to camp, they can remove it."

"It'll be too late then. They will know where the new camp is and they will come again and torture more people; people who know where the Montana camp is."

He walked over towards me and ran a finger gently down my throat. "I'm not leaving you here, Willow. I should've never let you go back to the Dominion by yourself in the first place."

"I did it though, Finn. I brought Brice home."

He smiled. "Yes, you did. My Willow warrior. You are incredible. Once we have you safe, you will have to tell me about all of your special gifts, like how you could talk to me when you were in the Dominion and I was at camp."

"I will. We need to get Brice loaded into the OHV. He won't be able to climb into Bernice. They broke his hands, too."

I followed Finn over to the passenger side of the

truck. Brice had already swung his legs out and was resting on the door frame. He was exhausted and in a lot of pain. I was amazed at his strength and resilience. He had kept up with me when we were escaping the CSS building. I could see now how large of a toll that taken on his body.

Finn wrapped Brice's arm around his shoulders and he helped him get into the back seat of the OHV. A woman started to assess his wounds and began pulling equipment out of her pack. She glanced over at us. "We need to get him back to base as soon as possible. He's got infection in the exposed muscle and I need to get him cleaned up and the bones put back in place before further growth occurs."

I placed my hand on Finn's muscular arm. "Take my brother home to safety."

He shook his head. "I'm not leaving you again." He turned towards the driver of the OHV. "Get back to camp and let Duncan and the others know that Willow and I are going to the old Crow's camp. Send another medical team there. Willow has a tracking device in her throat and we need to get it removed before we can enter the new camp."

The driver nodded and turned the OHV around. Several headlights flickered on behind Bernice, turning to follow Brice's OHV.

"How many Crows came with you?"

"Just about twenty. We weren't sure if you were going to be followed or not."

"I thought I was going to be until I heard Aurysia, Derek and Bradlee talking. That's how I found out about the tracking device and that they want to know where the camp in Montana is."

"Let's get back to the old camp. We can sleep in the combat cave until the team arrives. I packed food and water into the ACV."

"Okay, let me get the truck off of the road and into the brush."

"No, we will light it up right now just in case they changed their minds and followed. Having it block the road will deter them for a little bit."

I nodded and stepped back from the truck while Finn covered it with petrol and lit it on fire. We climbed into Bernice and headed towards the destroyed camp. Since they already knew where it was, there was no fear of us being there. I didn't think they would come after me anyway. They thought they had me under their thumb.

We pulled into the camp before midnight and all of my remaining energy evaporated from my body. It had been a long day and even longer night. All I wanted to do was sleep and now that Brice was safe,

I knew I could get the rest that had been eluding me since he was taken.

Finn and I agreed to sleep at my house since it had the least amount of damage. My room was destroyed, and I didn't feel comfortable sleeping in my parent's bed, so we righted the couches in the living room and grabbed blankets out of the closet. My grandmother's quilt slipped down from the shelf and I caught the heavy fabric in my arms. I hadn't seen it since I was a child and my breath hitched in my chest. I missed both her and my mother terribly.

I laid down on the couch and covered my body with her quilt, snuggling down into it. I glanced over at Finn who was lying on his side watching me. "What are you thinking of?"

"I'm thinking of what an idiot I was to ever agree to let you go back into the Dominion without me. I'm thinking that I think it took a miracle for you to rescue Brice and get out of there alive. I'm thinking I never want to let you out of my sight again and that I missed you."

I couldn't stop the grin that covered my face. "I missed you too, Finn. I have so much to tell you and so many new things that I've learned, not only about myself but about my history."

"I'll look forward to hearing about it then, in

the morning. You need to get some sleep if you can, Willow."

I murmured my agreement, but I wasn't sure if it was out loud or not, the darkness weighed my eyes closed and my mind slipped off with it like thieves in the night.

EIGHT

THE SMELL OF BACON TICKLED my nose and brought my mind back to consciousness. I started to rise but winced as I realized my muscles were sore and stiff. Long term adrenaline rushes definitely had their drawbacks.

Swinging my legs off the side of the couch, I saw that Finn's body was absent from the other one. I padded lightly into the kitchen and found him with his back towards me in front of the stove. He whistled a cheery tune as he turned the bacon. I saw a bowl filled with white batter and assumed it was pancakes. My stomach growled in excited anticipation.

"Where did you get the food?"

He whirled with a spatula in hand and I held back a giggle. He had a flour streak down the middle of his forehead and another up the side of his cheek.

"You snuck up on me," he chuckled. "I'm not used to that."

I stuck out my foot and wiggled my toes. "No shoes. Bare feet are quieter."

He frowned at my foot. "You need to wear your shoes in here. There's a lot of broken things from the soldiers. I don't want you to step on anything and cut yourself."

I saluted him sternly. "Yes sir."

He sighed heavily and put the spatula down. Walking over towards me he grabbed my hand and pulled me into his arms. "I'm sorry. I don't mean to be a dictator," he brushed some of my hair off my face. "I thought I lost you and it scared me to death. I don't want to see you hurt...ever."

His hand stayed on the side of my face and I leaned into it, closing my eyes and appreciating the warmth he created within me. I opened my eyes, wanting to see his beautiful green ones. "I don't want to see you hurt either, so I guess we will both be careful from here on out."

He smiled as he gazed down at me. "From here on out." He lowered his head towards mine and I felt my pulse begin to race. Was he really going to kiss me? Here?

I didn't care and when I felt his lips touch mine, my chest hitched with excitement. The kiss was warm, soft and his breath tasted minty.

A loud screeching startled us both and we whirled towards the noise. The bacon was burning on the stove and the smoke detector in the corner of the kitchen was warning everyone with ears. I heard Finn swear as he raced over and removed the skillet from the burner. I grabbed the broom and beat the detector to its death, its quiet body lying on the floor.

"Well that's one way to silence the dang thing."

I smiled at Finn and nodded. "First time I've ever heard it. Mom was great in the kitchen."

"I wish I could've been around to try some of her meals."

"Me too. Except maybe then you'd have high expectations for me and I'm not that great in the kitchen."

"Well it's just your luck that I *am* great in the kitchen."

I glanced over his shoulder and raised an eyebrow. "Really?"

"He snapped the towel towards me. "I'm not usually distracted."

I felt coy with the teasing. "Were you distracted, Finn?"

He growled and moved towards me. I laughed and jumped away from him, placing the dining room table between us. "I thought you were making breakfast for us? I'm starving and haven't eaten since yesterday when I swallowed that tracker pastry."

He shook his head. "I'll make you breakfast but this isn't over. Not by a long shot."

"I'm going to hold you to that." I loved our banter and was having fun, but I knew we needed to get the day started. We had to get the tracking chip removed from my throat.

I made my way carefully to the bathroom and quickly brushed my teeth. I heard panting in my ear and tickling breath tease the back of my neck. I giggled and swiped Finn away but froze when my hand didn't come into contact with him. Feeling my heart start to pound, I looked up in the mirror, fearful of what I *wouldn't* see. There was no one behind me.

As I continued to stare, I saw my hair move gently, as if a breeze had picked up the lighter tendrils and played with them delicately. There weren't any windows open in the bathroom and nothing that would stir the air in the house.

Bradlee appeared in the mirror, or an image of him.

He was as blue and wispy as the constabulary soldiers had been when we had first visited the camp after the attack. He wasn't wearing combat attire and he didn't appear to be armed. I watched, mesmerized by his movie.

I noticed that the trees were bare, and the sun was shining but I could see his breath as he climbed. This wasn't a vision from the past. When the Dominion had attacked the camp, it had been late October and there were still colorful leaves on the trees.

I dropped the toothbrush and grabbed the towel, wiping my mouth as I barreled into the kitchen. "Finn! Bradlee is on his way here."

Finn's eyes enlarged as he sat the plate of pancakes down onto the table. "Are you sure?"

"Yes, I saw him in the mirror just now."

A scowl crossed between his eyes. "What do you mean you saw him in the mirror?"

"Do you remember how I saw the wisps and fragments of the soldiers who destroyed the Crow's camp? He was like that only the trees were bare, the sun was shining and I could see his breath. It wasn't from the past."

He marched towards the living room, picking up a pistol and tucking it in the back waistband of his pants. "Could it be a future possibility, like when you saw them attack the camp the first time?"

I shook my head, "I don't think so. I have the feeling like he's going to be here...now." I grabbed my quiver and slung it over my shoulder as we were walking towards the door.

"Did you see anyone with him?"

"No, I think he's alone."

"What is he thinking? Why is he coming back here?"

I felt pale and sick. "It's my tracker. They know where I'm at. He's come to get me and take me back to the Dominion."

"Over my dead body," he turned and gently grabbed my chin, lifting my face towards his. "Nobody is going to take you away from me again, Willow. Nobody."

I smiled softly, hoping that he could keep that promise but I knew from experience that the Dominion would go to any lengths to get what they wanted.

We made our way to the center of camp and foraged through the rubble to see if there were any tools or weapons that had been missed. Neither one of us were expecting to find anything and we both knew it was a way to waste time while we waited...waited for either Bradlee to show up and announce his intentions or for the Crow IT and medical team to show up and extract my transmitter. There was no way I would go back to the temporary camp and expose the Crows.

I heard him before I saw him, coming in from the direction of Angel Falls and the Domination Lookout. I pulled my bow and nocked an arrow, aiming it for his heart. Finn hadn't seen him yet; he was still poking through the debris.

"What are you doing here, Bradlee?" I was surprised at how strong my voice sounded.

Finn whirled and aimed his pistol at him.

Bradlee lifted his hands in surrender and slowed his pace. "I'm here as a friend, Willow. I promise."

"I don't need any more friends, Bradlee. Especially ones like you."

"Willow, please, hear me out," he pleaded.

The image of Brice's face popped into my mind and I took an angry step towards him. "Why should I? You took my brother, let the Dominion torture him and left him to rot. You corrupted my father and plotted with him to destroy the Crows and me along with them. You had a hand in killing my mother. *Why* do you think I should even give you the time of day, let alone hear you out," my anger was rising and I marched towards him. I threw my bow down and pulled out my knife. Stepping up into his face, I held it up to his neck; the sharpened blade dimpling his flesh.

"Give me one good reason why I shouldn't slit your throat right now this minute."

I saw fear take residence in his eyes and his mouth started twitching but no words came out. I pushed the blade a little more and a thin line of blood appeared beneath the blade.

"Will. Hear him out before we kill him."

Finn's soothing voice was right behind me and I could feel his breath on my neck.

I stepped back, slightly surprised that I didn't bump into Finn, but I didn't take my eyes off of Bradlee. "You have less than ninety seconds to talk."

"I want to help. I can see now how messed up the Dominion is."

I couldn't stop the snort that forced its way from my nose.

"It's true. The year I lived among the Crows and worked with Duncan and Brice was the best year I'd ever had. The Crows work with a fairness and compassion that I have never known. I never experienced such a camaraderie as when I was here. I can see now why you choose to live with them."

"And that's why you tortured Brice and conspired with my Dad to have me killed?"

"No, it wasn't supposed to happen that way. They said they wanted you to figure out your gifts and when we couldn't convince you to come back within the fold, taking Brice was a way to get you back," he took a deep breath and took a tentative step forward. "And it worked. You came back. But you have gifts that even your father didn't know about."

I felt like I had been sucker punched. "My dad knew about my gifts? How? I didn't even know about my gifts until after we got here."

"Your mother had gifts and your father knew about them. He knew they came from your mother's side and were passed down genetically. He had hoped that there had been some talents in his lineage and when combined, would create an incredibly talented child. It failed with Aurysia. She has no gifts whatsoever. But his other daughter is turning into a prodigy unlike any of her predecessors."

"You have a sister?"

I turned towards Finn, finally taking my eyes off of Bradlee. "Supposedly my father had an affair with Bernadette Winters and Aurysia is the result of that. I have yet to verify that information," I hesitated a moment, trying to get the scrambled thoughts running through my mind in order. "though she does have the same colored eyes as me."

"Holy mother of all that's good," Finn ran a hand

over his face. "What else did you learn while you were there?"

"I learned that they forcibly sterilize parents who don't conform to the Dominion rules and that they use the children to manipulate adults to bend to their will," I shook my head. "And I don't have proof yet, but I don't think the children are ever returned to their family. I think they are permanently in the system and used for experiments."

Finn glared at Bradlee. "Is this true?"

Bradlee shrugged his shoulders. "They are small sacrifices for the greater good."

I lunged forward and punched him in the gut. "Small sacrifices? They are someone's daughter or son. Innocent lives being ripped away from the people who love them for *government* progress?"

Bradlee doubled over, coughing and spitting. "Willow. I want to help. I promise. I was the one who let all of the Addictors and Payment Repudiators out so you and Brice could get away."

"How and why am I supposed to believe you? You probably have a tracker inside of you and Derek and his covey are already on their way."

"I don't. They don't know I left. I falsified travel programs so I could make it here without detection. They probably know I'm gone now but not where I went."

Finn stepped forward. "It wouldn't take rocket science to figure out where you went."

"They wouldn't suspect here. I betrayed the Crows and brought in Willow's brother. They would probably think I'd be killed if I came back."

"Which is what I vote for," I couldn't help the snide remark that slid out.

Engines broke the silence and all of us turned to see who was coming. Several OHVs broke through the tree line and headed towards us. From the attire, I could tell they were Crows. Finn waved them over and the riders of the front OHVs drew their guns when they saw Bradlee. Bradlee instinctively held up his hands again, showing submission.

They stopped next to us and several members climbed out as Finn greeted them and filled them in on what was going on. I stepped towards them when I felt Bradlee grab my arm and turn me towards him.

"I want to stop all of this, Willow. The Neonate Asylum, Payment Repudiators, Addictors and now Bernadette pushing for IV infused meals. The Dominion is becoming more corrupt and they need to be stopped." He stared so intently into my eyes. I didn't get the impression that he was hiding anything from me. He honestly seemed disgusted with the Dominion regulation.

I shook my arm from his grip and leaned towards him. "If you don't have a tracking device on you, we will see about trusting you. Right now, I don't trust you at all."

I turned and walked away. I wasn't concerned about if Bradlee left or not. He didn't know where the new camp was so he could either stay with us or he could go back to the Dominion. At this point, I didn't care.

"Willow, this is Joni. You might have remembered her training with us when you first arrived at camp."

I smiled at the familiar, freckled brunette. "I do remember. How are you doing, Joni? Why did you leave the scout team?"

"I fell in love with medicine and technology. Duncan was very supportive of my decision and helped guide me."

She had a warm smile and I was glad she was the one who was going to take care of my tracking problem. "Is this going to hurt?" I saw her smile fall slightly and my stomach immediately clenched.

"It depends on what we find. We need to scan you first and find out where it is. Once we are able to identify what kind of tracking device it is we will be able to determine how to remove it or negate it."

I nodded then glanced over at Bradlee. "I need you

to scan him first. Everything. His clothes, his body. Everywhere that they could possibly hide a tracker."

She glanced up at Finn which slightly irritated me. I understood that Finn was in charge of security and the scout team, but I was the one who was requesting that Bradlee be scanned. I was still part of the Crows.

Finn nodded at Joni. "Willow is equal to me in ranking. Whatever she requests needs to be done."

Joni glanced over at me and shrugged apologetically, her face bright red. "Sorry, Willow. I didn't know."

I smiled but I know it didn't reach my eyes. "Thanks, let's just get Bradlee scanned so we can figure out what to do with me."

She walked back to the OHV and pulled out a large, black briefcase. I brought Bradlee closer to the vehicles so we could work quickly and efficiently. I didn't want to be here another night and I wanted to see how Brice was doing.

Joni began to scan Bradlee's body, making sure to cover every crevice. She had him take off his jacket and another Crow scanned it for any bugs or devices. After ten minutes, she turned to me and shook her head. "I can't find any trackers either on his person or inside. Unless the Dominion have come up with a new type of device, he's clean."

I hated the way Bradlee was smiling at me. It was a smug, I-told-you-so expression that I wanted to punch off of his face. Forget about slapping. I turned towards Joni and nodded. "Okay, now it's my turn."

She began to run the scanner over my body and just as Aurysia had spouted, there was one lodged in my throat. I didn't like the look Joni shot at Finn. "What? What is wrong?"

She shook her head, "This is a new type of tracker, one I'm not familiar with so I don't know what reactors it has programmed into it."

I swallowed involuntary. My imagination made it seem like I could feel the tracker in my throat. "What do you mean, reactors?"

"Like with the PIMs. If you try to remove them, they detonate. I don't know if this is a submissive tracker or a reactive one."

Bradlee came to stand next to me. "May I see which one it is? I can help."

Joni looked at me and I nodded. He scanned over my throat again and I saw his eyes squinch. I could tell it wasn't good.

"What is it, Bradlee?"

He met my gaze. "It's a Three Strikes tracker."

"What is a Three Strikes tracker?"

He took a deep breath. "They are usually inserted

into repeat Addictors who don't comply after the first two punishments."

Finn stood slightly behind me. "What are the first two punishments?"

"They test positive for synthetic drugs the kids are taken away while the parents get clean. The second time they kids are taken away permanently and the parents are sterilized so they can't have any more kids," Bradlee explained.

I could tell where this was going and I didn't like it. "And what's the last punishment?"

"The tracker is installed when they are sterilized and if it detects synthetic drugs in your system, it detonates wherever it is located at. So it could be a slow death or a fast one, depending on where the device is located."

Finn stepped in front of me and grabbed the front of Bradlee's shirt. "What does that mean for Willow?"

"It has to be removed without any drugs in her system."

My vision wavered slightly as his words sunk in. I would have to be awake and no numbing medication to remove the tracker.

"We would have to take her back to the camp and strap her down," Joni interrupted. "We couldn't risk her jerking while we were trying to extract it."

"Willow can't have her throat cut open to have

the tracker removed without something to numb the area and cut the pain," Finn argued, releasing Bradlee and standing beside me again.

Everyone was talking around me and over me like I wasn't there. I was the one with the device in their body. Brice's face came to my mind and I stood up straighter, knowing what needed to be done.

"I'm *not* going back to camp with this thing in my body and if it means I have to have it removed while I'm awake, then so be it," I turned towards Finn. "It'll be fine and needs to be done." I whirled on Bradlee accusingly. "Brice didn't have any synthetic drugs when they detonated his PIM, did he?"

I saw Bradlee flinch and I was glad my words had the desired effect on him. He shook his head and dropped his eyes.

I turned back towards Joni and Finn. "See? People survive. Brice had much more destruction done and I'm sure Joni has a small device to remove it."

"I...," she was shaking her head and took a step back.

I didn't like her hesitation. "What? You what?"

"I've never removed one of these before. I haven't even seen them so I'm not confident in removing it."

"Well we all have to start somewhere, right? I might as well be your first on this type."

"Let me. I helped design them. I know all about them."

Finn lunged forward. "You are not *touching* her."

I put my arm across Finn's chest and stopped him. "If he knows about these things, he's the best chance I have." I turned towards Bradlee, holding his brilliant blue eyes with my lavender ones. "A unicorn, right?"

His face softened and he nodded. "A beautiful and rare unicorn."

Joni's face held obvious relief. "Great! We need to find a clean area to lay her down on. The medical house here was destroyed so somewhere else will have to work."

"The bat cave had the rehabilitation area we can use."

Bradlee chuckled, "Bat cave?"

I shrugged slightly, glad to have the mood lighten. "I hated calling it the combat cave. Sounds so boring. Bat cave makes it sound mysterious and superhero-like."

Finn touched my shoulder, pulling me from the others. "I don't like this, Willow."

I caressed the side of his face softly. "I don't either, but we don't have much of a choice. I can't go back to the camp with this thing in my body and we can't use any synthetic drugs."

"Yeah, but do you really trust Bradlee?"

"No, but do I have a choice?"

He closed his eyes and rested his forehead against mine. I closed my own and inhaled his minty breath. "It'll be okay, Finn. And if I end up exploding, you can kill Bradlee." I couldn't help the giggle that slipped from me. I know it was a reaction to the stress, but it felt good anyway.

Finn pulled back, his green eyes twinkling. "You sure are something special, Willow Danner. You know that, don't you?"

I rolled my eyes. "So everyone keeps telling me. Took eighteen years for people to finally realize it."

I cleared my throat and turned towards Bradlee and Joni. "Okay, let's get this done. I want to go back to the camp so this thing needs to go now."

NINE

IT WAS AMAZING WATCHING JONI'S crew clean and sanitize the area my surgery was going to be performed. They worked meticulously and fluidly, never getting in another's way. It was only twenty minutes before they were ready for me and Joni patted the table she wanted me on.

I took a deep breath and forced my feet to move. Finn grabbed my hand, squeezing it as he walked with me towards the table. I hopped up and lay down on my back.

Finn looked down at me and smiled. "I'll be right here holding your hand. Are you absolutely sure about this?"

I smiled and nodded. "I'm sure. I want to get back to my crow family and besides," I closed my eyes and pictured my mother's beautiful face. "I'm a falcon. We can handle anything, even death if it's required."

Before Finn had a chance to say anything, Bradlee stepped up and placed a hand on my shoulder. "You ready?"

I opened my eyes and stared at him. This was the man who tore apart my family and betrayed my faction. Could I really trust him? If what he said about the Three Strikes sensor was true, he could detonate it and eliminate me right here and now. My life was literally in his hands.

"I am," I breathed.

"Finn, you need to give me room so go stand over there."

"I'm not going anywhere."

"Then at least stand on the other side so I have room to work and there won't be the risk of you bumping me."

"Finn, Bradlee! Stop arguing and focus on Willow."

I was impressed with Joni's authoritative tone and sent her a thankful smile. I was glad she was on my side.

"I need to strap your forehead down to help keep

you from moving. Where the sensor is located is the side of your esophagus. I can't have you move at all once I start cutting, do you understand?"

I nodded and swallowed.

He grabbed the laser cutter and hovered over me. I focused on his blue eyes to give me a distraction. His eyes were so vocal and told a story if one actually took the time to pay attention. I had noticed the first time I had dreamt of his eyes. They were cold and hard that time; death was the only purpose. When we practiced hand-to-hand combat, they were playful and friendly. Today they were calm and determined. It eased my mind.

I heard the sizzle before I felt the burn. It felt like a hot knife was slicing through my skin and I felt wetness leak from the corners of my eyes.

"You are doing great, Willow. I'm almost through the last layer of skin and muscle."

Joni cleared her throat and I saw her shadow move over me to get a closer look. "You haven't hit the submucosa yet?"

"Just now and getting ready to cut the mucosa now. Please have the extractor ready."

I saw his eyes widen slightly and saw the concern there. I wanted desperately to ask what was wrong but knew I couldn't risk the movement of my throat.

He glanced at me and winked. "It's all good, Willow. Just a slight hiccup but nothing I can't handle."

He looked up at Joni. "I'm going to need you to hold the incision open a little wider. See where the lead leg is longer? It's hooked into the mucosa lining which is why it never went down into her stomach."

"Can't you cut the leg off?"

He shook his head. "These are made to detonate if there's any tampering to them. I need to unhook it before I can remove it."

The pain in my throat intensified as they stretched the opening wider. I felt each tug and resisted the urge to cough and dislodge the painful object. I squeezed my hands into a fist and shut my eyes to the pain. My mind was screaming at me to make them stop and I wasn't sure how long I could hold off the urge to begin thrashing and screaming for them to quit.

I felt someone grab my hand and squeeze it tight. I squeezed back, focusing on the heat of connection with that person. My person. Finn.

"Got it. Now let's get her sealed up. Willow?"

I opened my eyes and looked at Bradlee.

"I got it out and now I need to close you up. I'm going to place two small stitches in the submucosa and then I'll seal your skin with dermal glue. You'll have a tiny little scar when I'm done but nothing too big."

I felt the needle flow through my flesh and squeezed Finn's hand harder. The pain was excruciating.

"If the sensor is out why can't you numb her now?" Finn's voice was filled with anger and frustration.

"By the time the numbing medicine kicks in, I'll have her sewn up. The longer we leave it open and exposed the greater the increase of infection. I'm almost done if you'd let me focus, Finn."

The silence became deafening and I felt every pull and tug Bradlee made on my body. I knew it was probably only minutes, but it felt like years before he finally squeezed my shoulder.

"It's done, Willow. It's out."

Both he and Finn helped me to a sitting position.

"I don't want you to try and talk for a few days, and only liquids are a part of your diet for the next forty-eight hours. We don't want to rip those stitches."

I nodded and tentatively touched the injured area. It was sore and I could feel the smooth, rigid glue. I slid down, wary of my legs when I felt them give a little.

Finn shot by my side. "Easy Willow. You just had surgery without the benefit of any drugs."

I put my hand up and glared at him. I was fine

and wanted to tell him so but couldn't. All I wanted to do was get back to camp and see how my brother was doing. I looked towards the cave entrance and pointed before attempting to stomp away. After the first jolt reminded me of my injury, I eased my exit and focused on getting to the OHVs without falling. I didn't bother to look back to see if the others were coming. I'd leave without them if I had to.

I climbed into the backseat of the OHV I had ridden over in. The others came out carrying various pieces of the equipment they had just used on me. Bradlee made the move to sit beside me in the back but Finn stopped him.

"I don't think so, Bradlee. You don't get that right."

Bradlee turned and squared up to him. "I think I have earned that right and I need to keep an eye on her incision. If it splits open during the ride or she starts to show signs of infection, I'll be able to catch it quicker than you."

"Joni can catch it just as fast. You can sit somewhere else and I'll drive."

Joni eyed the two of them, unsure what to do before she slid in the seat beside me. "How do you deal with all of the testosterone that those two put out?" she whispered.

I looked at her and rolled my eyes.

She giggled and nodded. "Yeah, that's what I thought. You good? The bumps are going to hurt like hell. I can give you a shot of Oxytanyl. It won't put you out, but it'll make the pain go away until we get to camp."

I nodded, wanting to be free of the sharp burning pain in my throat that intensified with every swallow.

"Make sure you keep an eye on her blood pressure if she's never taken it before," Bradlee warned.

"Yep, hooking her up now." Joni attached adhesive tabs on my neck and wrist. She pulled out a syringe and checked the vial before turning to me. "Ready? I'm just going to inject this into your arm. It'll burn as it's going in but will go away."

I nodded again and looked away. I could stitch up Finn's bloody arm and see Brice's face torn up but I had an issue with needles; especially when they were going into me. I jumped slightly as the burning sensation radiated out underneath my flesh but within seconds I didn't care. Heat flooded my body, washing away any sore muscles and the pain in my throat. I glanced at Joni and smiled.

"Okay guys, she's in La La Land. We have about four hours before this stuff wears off so hit it."

The others had climbed into their OHVs and we

were bouncing along the trails that would take us to the new camp. I allowed my mind to wander on its own, enjoying the momentary feeling of being powerless but in trusted hands.

Memories of my childhood danced and twirled before me and for the first time I observed from the position of an outsider instead of from within. I saw the relationship between my brother and I and the bond that we had even though at times we swore we hated each other. I saw how my mother and father fought often and times he would go off to work in the evenings, leaving us kids with Mom. I frowned at that memory because we worked our leased land from the Dominion. It was a job we did as a family so where was he going in the evenings? Why didn't we go with him?

The memories continued on, oblivious to my desire to delve into that particular memory. Escaping the Dominion and the first time I experienced one of my developing gifts, hearing the drone heading towards us before anyone else had heard it. I shuddered slightly thinking of what would've happened had I not heard it.

Meeting Finn for the first time in the forest and hearing him and Duncan talking before they surprised us. He hadn't trusted me back then and honestly, I couldn't blame him. He had been betrayed by those close to him. I understood the pain of that betrayal. My father's maniacal face came so strong into my vision that I jumped slightly. If it hadn't been for my mother, he would have killed me. I tried to argue with myself on that point but no matter which way I tried to look at it, I couldn't see any other choice he would've had.

That pain was sharp and even the drugs couldn't ease it. My own father, who taught me the importance of freedom, and the importance of being a Crow, would've ended my life. I thought I was his everything, his little girl. Little girl...

Was that where he was going in the evenings? To go see his other daughter? Did he stay in touch with Bernadette and Aurysia while we were still living in the Dominion? Did Mom know?

Aurysia's fair features floated before me, her condescending look marring her otherwise beautiful face. We shared a father and the same color of eyes, but it appeared that was all we shared.

"Why do you hate me so much?" my mind asked the wavering image of my sister.

"Because he loved you more."

I froze, unsure if this was a side effect of the pain medicine or if I had accidently connected with her.

"How is it that not only you got our father, but you inherited all of these incredible gifts too? I'm guessing this is another one; being able to talk to people without any device."

"I'm not sure if I'm really communicating with you or if it's an effect of the pain meds," I saw her face flicker for a moment with doubt. "Yeah," I continued. "I found your sensor and we removed it. You'll never find the camp. This one *or* the one in Montana."

"You bi..."

"Nope, I'm not that. I'm a Gyrfalcon and you are not. Bloodlines passed down through my *mother's* side. For as long as I'm alive, the Dominion will have an enemy."

"The Crows will never win. We are too powerful and far more advanced than any of you will ever be."

"Haven't you heard, sister? The Crows are gone, scattered like little sparrows. What's taking their place are falcons. We are diverse, unrelenting and formidable. You may think you know when we are coming but you never will. Not until it's too late."

She screamed in fury, striking out as if trying to hit me through our distance. I laughed as I released her image and focused on the landscape around me. We weren't but an hour away from the camp and I was surprised. Had I been talking with Aurysia that long?

It didn't matter. We were almost there and the meds were wearing off; the throbbing in my throat beginning to escalate again.

Joni tapped me on the shoulder and handed me a water bottle. "Your blood pressure is rising again. You need to stay hydrated and relax. You are really anxious right now."

I smiled. If she only knew.

TEN

JENNIFER WAS THE FIRST ONE to practically pull me out of the OHV and embrace me tightly. "Girl, you better never do that again. When Duncan announced you had gone back into the Dominion... *alone* to get Brice, I was madder than a wet hen. You always have the Crows at your back. We are a faction; we are family."

I saw Duncan standing back allowing Jennifer to admonish me. His smile told me that he agreed with everything she was saying but I knew he understood. When she finally released me, he moved forward and pulled me into a hug.

"It's good to have you back, kiddo." He pulled

back and studied my throat. "Looks like Bradlee did a good job."

I nodded and turned when I heard the boos and hisses from the crowd. Bradlee was getting out of the OHV while Finn came out from the other side. They began throwing sticks and rocks at him, several of them hitting their mark. I pulled away from Duncan and jumped up angrily on the OHV, waving my hands. The crowd fell silent and Finn climbed up to stand beside me.

"Bradlee is the one who helped Willow and Brice escape. He's also the one who removed the tracker in Willow's throat. He is sorry for betraying the Crows and wants to show his allegiance to us."

At the murmuring of the crowd, I elbowed Finn and nodded towards the crowd.

"Willow wants you to know that while she doesn't trust him fully at this time, she's willing to allow him to prove himself. We will all watch him, with careful and scrutinous eyes, until the time comes that we truly trust him again."

I stared at the crowd, daring them to question my decision. They had questioned me before and it almost cost all of us our lives. I wouldn't let them forget that. I wouldn't doubt myself anymore, neither would I allow anyone else.

I gently jumped down from the OHV, holding my throat. Turning towards Finn, I whispered softly, wincing at the pain. "Take me to Brice."

"You need to get some rest," he argued.

I grimaced and hit my fist in my other hand. I wasn't going to argue with him.

He rolled his eyes. "Fine."

He pushed through the crowd and headed towards the middle of camp. I followed closely behind, smiling at those who welcomed me and patted me on the back.

Finn stopped in front of the recovery house and opened the door for me. I stepped through and saw Brice lying on one of the far beds, the side of his face bandaged. A young man I didn't recognize was standing near him, writing something down on a pad of paper. He glanced at me when he heard the door open. He stepped forward and held out his hand.

"You must be Willow, Brice's sister. I'm Jason Stone. I'm one of the docs up in the Montana faction."

I cocked my head, surprised to meet someone from the infamous Crow camp.

He glanced at my throat and met my eyes. "It looks like you had a little problem getting home."

"She swallowed a Three Strikes Sensor and Bradlee took it out about three hours ago."

Jason looked over my shoulder, spotting Finn. "Bradlee is here?"

"Yes. He said he's defected from the Dominion and wants to prove himself. Willow insisted he remove the tracker before she would come back to camp, in order to keep the rest of us safe."

Jason's brown eyes met mine and he stared at me incredulously. "I've heard of your gifts and talents; I just hadn't realized how determined you truly are."

"She has more talents than what we even knew before she left."

I turned and glared at Finn, trying to tell him not to say any more. I didn't want to be the Dominion's guinea pig and I didn't want to be the Crow's either.

Finn looked properly chastised and closed his mouth. He stepped further into the room and nodded towards Brice. "How is he doing?"

Jason turned back towards his patient. "He's very lucky to be alive. The PIM must have been defective because the mandible is still there. It's in pieces but still there. Brice should've either lost the entire side of his jaw or the top of his head. I can rebuild the bone and put his jaw back in place. With quite a few surgeries, I will be able to close up his cheek. He will always have scars and it will take time, but he will be able to eat and speak normally, eventually."

"I can get him back to normal sooner."

Three sets of eyes turned towards the intruder standing in the doorway. Once again, Bradlee had intruded without being asked or given permission.

Finn lunged towards him to shove him out but Bradlee held out his hand towards me. "Willow! I know how to make your brother better. I promise. It's one way I can start to make up for what I've done."

"Finn," I called out, my throat protesting at the vibration and pressure.

He stopped and turned towards me, murder in his eyes. "You trusted him with your life and now you're going to trust him with Brice's?"

I nodded and saw him deflate before me. He glared at Bradlee before pushing past him, hitting Bradlee's shoulder with his own.

Bradlee rubbed his shoulder as he watched Finn leave the building. When he was sure he was gone, he walked towards me. "I've been studying bone and muscle regeneration while at the Dominion. My IT work with Duncan was fun and I enjoyed it, but my main focus of training has always been a combination of medicine and technology. I can have his jaw reset, regrown and the muscles in his cheek back to normal within three weeks."

Jason moved towards Bradlee. "I take it you

are Bradlee?" When Bradlee nodded, Jason shook his head. "While I'm impressed with your work on Willow, I won't let you give her *or* Brice false hope. What you are suggesting is impossible."

"With all due respect..."

"Jason. Dr. Jason Stone."

"With all due respect, *doctor*, we have been working on gene and cell regeneration for quite a while and we've had some impressive breakthroughs the past six months." He turned towards me and glanced at my throat. "I can prove it to you. If you let me, with some of the equipment here I will heal your throat." He stepped closer to me and I could smell his musky scent. "I need you to trust me again, Will."

My body shuddered and I wasn't sure why. I glanced up at him, his blue eyes boring so intensely I felt like he was looking into my essence. I nodded and he smiled. He mouthed thank you before looking up at Jason.

"I need to see all of the equipment you have here. And if you're up to it, I'd like your help, too."

Jason glanced at me and I nodded. If I was going to be a guinea pig *this* time, he might as well be a part of it. Especially if what he learned on me could heal Brice faster.

The two men began to gather equipment, talking

animatedly about things that I hadn't heard of. I moved towards Brice and sat down on the stool that was beside his bed. He was lying on his back, his eyes closed. I touched his shoulder softly so I wouldn't wake him. He opened his eyes and looked at me. The lines at the corners of his eyes crinkled and I saw his cheeks lift slightly.

I mouthed the words, *I love you,* and I saw a tear slip from his eye. I wiped it away knowing he wanted to say the same but the damage to his jaw prevented it. I sat there smiling at him and stroking his hair like Mom had done to us when we snuggled on the couch to listen to her or Dad's tales of what America had been like before the war.

"Willow, we are ready for you."

I smiled at Brice and kissed his forehead as I rose. Turning towards Bradlee and Jason, I waited for them to tell me where they wanted me.

Bradlee moved towards the adjoining room and Jason waited for me to pass through before following. A large surgical table was in the middle of a light blue room. The windows were sealed off and a tray of stainless-steel tools lay beside the bed. I swallowed, ignoring the pain. I sat down on the table and scooted back.

"I need you to remove your jacket and your shirt.

You can leave your bra on but cover up with the gown and tie it towards the back."

Jason chuckled. "Years of growing technology and we haven't come up with a better gown system."

I smiled, appreciating his attempt to lighten the mood. I waited until both of them left and closed the door before stripping down. I didn't know how long they were going to give me and since I couldn't talk to let them know I was covered; I didn't want to be exposed.

Quickly donning the gown and tying it behind my neck, I just finished when there was a light knock at the door and Jason tentatively opened the door.

"All decent?" He glanced in cautiously, and when he saw I was covered, opened the door the rest of the way.

Bradlee came in and placed his hand on my knee. "Okay. I want to go through exactly what I'm going to do so you know. There will be no surprises, Willow, and when you wake up you will be able to talk, there won't be any pain and you won't have any scar on your throat."

I nodded and he proceeded to explain what he was going to do. Jason was listening intently. I didn't understand half of the terms he used but the basic gist I got was that he was going to take some of my skin cells from inside my nose, rapidly grow them and plant them on the inside and outside of my throat. Another tool was going to promote growth of the new cells to attach to my existing cells and it was going to heal me both inside and out.

"If that sounds okay to you and you want to proceed, nod your head."

I nodded and he helped me lay down on the table.

"You don't have to be awake for it this time, Willow. You will go to sleep and when you wake up, you will be all done."

He placed a mask over my mouth and nose, and I breathed deeply. I felt my mind slip from my body and I allowed the release. Just before darkness claimed me, I wondered if this was what death felt like.

"How in the hell could you allow him to do a procedure on Willow? And why didn't anyone ask me about it?"

The yelling pierced through the foggy darkness and I slowly opened my eyes. Finn was super mad and I pitied the object of his anger.

"Because I was there the entire time watching," Jason's calm voice replied.

"I didn't realize *you* were designated Willow's

keeper," Bradlee's voice dripped venom. "And if you are, where were you when she went into the Dominion alone?"

Their yelling was starting a pounding throb at my temples and I attempted to sit up, irritation flooding my body. "Boys."

All three heads turned in my direction. Finn moved to my side, helping support me into a sitting position.

"Are you alright, Willow?"

"I'd be better if you would all stop yelling." I touched my throat, realizing it hadn't hurt when I spoke. I glanced up at Jason and Bradlee, smiling. "It doesn't hurt."

Bradlee beamed. "I told you it wouldn't. And you don't have a scar anymore either."

Jason moved towards me and stared at the spot on my throat. "It's absolutely incredible. I've never seen anything like it. This can help so many others."

"We should get started on Brice right away. Granted his injuries are more extreme so they will take longer to heal but I think we can have him back to normal within a week." He looked at me. "As long as it's okay with Willow and Brice."

"It's definitely okay with me."

Jason and Bradlee met each other with huge grins and left to go talk to Brice and make their plan.

I turned towards Finn. "This is a good thing, Finn. Why are you so angry?"

He brushed a strand of hair from my forehead but wouldn't meet my gaze. "How can you trust so easily, Willow? He betrayed us, betrayed you and your family. He was the spy trying to destroy the Crows."

"But he realizes he was wrong and recognizes that."

"People don't change that fast or that much."

I grabbed his chin and forced him to look at me. "Don't they, Finnian Sennet? I don't even resemble the girl I was less than a year ago and I probably won't recognize the woman I'll be a year from now, if I live that long. People can change and grow if they want to. I think Bradlee wants to."

He sighed and lightly kissed my lips. "I missed you, Willow Danner. Very much."

"I missed you too."

"It's almost dinner time and Jennifer and Mandy have been cooking up a storm in celebration of you and Brice coming home."

"Oh, yes. I've missed Jennifer's cooking and Mandy's baking. I didn't get to enjoy your breakfast this morning and I'm starving."

He helped me off the table. We moved into the next room and I made my way to Brice, who was actually sitting up watching Jason and Bradlee excitedly working.

"Brice, did they tell you what they are going to do?" I knelt before him and lifted my chin to expose my neck. "See? You can't even see the scar anymore."

He grabbed my hand and squeezed it.

"You will be back to normal in no time and I'll make sure Jason or Bradlee show you how to do all of this too so we can teach our own medical team how to do this."

I saw a shadow pass over his eyes.

"I'm still watching him, Brice but he is the one who helped us and healed me. Just like Dad changed sides and went to the Dominion, Bradlee might be on the side of us, the Falcons."

I saw him trying to mouth "crows", but I shook my head. "Mom explained how the Crow faction got its name but that doesn't fit us; not anymore. When the Dominion hit, we took flight like scared little sparrows. We weren't prepared, but that won't happen again. We are going back; we are freeing those who don't deserve imprisonment. We will strike with a force they have never seen before. I just need time to call us back together."

He stared at me like he had never seen me before. Maybe he hadn't. His little sister was gone. She had died when their mother and father had died. The woman who stood before him now was not afraid.

◆◆◆

I sat back and watched my faction eat, drink and celebrate. Mandy had hugged me so many times I thought she was going to snap my ribs. Jennifer had tried to fill my plate twice, but I couldn't eat anymore; my stomach was rebelling.

The campfire felt warm and though it was early in the evening, it was fully dark. Winter always held shorter daylight hours.

I sensed someone staring at me and as I scanned the faces in the flickering firelight, I caught Kathy glaring at me. I sighed and held my glass up in a toast, smiling. Some things didn't change. She still hated my guts despite my warning every one of the impending attack from the Dominion and having lead the Crows to safety.

Her glare was interrupted by someone hidden by the crowd. She smiled warmly and I was surprised by how pretty she really was when she wasn't glaring. I craned my neck to try and see who was the object of her pleasure, was when I saw the person sit down next to her. Finn.

I felt a stab of jealousy as I watched them converse, and while he didn't do anything that was untoward, I still felt the pain. What could he possibly have to say to her? He knew how much she liked him and how much she hated me for it.

"He still clueless about how much she likes him?"

I startled and tore my focus from Finn and Kathy to see Bradlee sit down next to me. I smiled slightly and returned my gaze to them. "No, he knows. She made it perfectly clear that I wasn't good enough for him and that he should be with her."

"And he's still talking with her? In front of you?" he shook his head and took a drink. "If you were my girl, I'd never let anyone distract me, and you'd never have reason to wonder."

I took a deep breath. I wasn't in the mood to get into a pissing contest between him and Finn. "Well, then I guess it's a good thing I'm not *your* girl." I stood up and looked down at him. "Thanks for healing me, Bradlee. Have a good night."

I turned and walked back to the cabin where Finnian and I were sleeping. I crawled into bed. Full from the delicious meal and exhausted from the past week, I longed to slip into a deep slumber.

"Willow?"

I kept my eyes shut, hoping Finn would just let me be and go to sleep. I wasn't in the mood to talk… about anything.

I sensed him looming over me and instinct wanted me to open my eyes. Sheer stubbornness kept them shut.

"I love you, Willow. I'm glad your home."

I didn't move even though everything inside of me screamed to tell him that I loved him too. My heart pounded with joy while my mind warned of being hurt and of possible betrayal if I let my guard down. Kathy's nasty glare came to mind and was what kept me silent.

I heard the cot squeak as Finn crawled into bed. I allowed my soul to sleep, promising to deal with my emotions at a later time.

ELEVEN

"NO! NO! I WANT MY mommy!" Inka screamed, throwing her little fists while mucus from her eyes and nose flew everywhere.

"Your parents don't care about you anymore. We are your family now and you must do what we tell you to do." A gaunt older woman attempted to grab at the writhing child.

"That's a lie! My mommy told me to *nevew* twust assium people. I'm her mini-me, that's what she called me. You lie!"

Inka bit the woman's hand who screamed and yanked it back. "It's pronounced asylum, you little brat. You don't want me to bring in Constable Derek, do you? You heard what he said he'll do if you behave this way anymore."

Inka's eyes grew wide and she stopped her fighting. "No, please don't call Contable Dewek. I'll be good, please don't hurt my wittle bwuver."

"That's better. Now come along with me like a good little girl and I'll make sure you can go see your brother this afternoon."

Yes ma'am, but I don't like the needles. They hurt so bad. Can't I eat like I used to? Just this once?"

"No, Inka. I've told you. We need to make sure this works so other people can benefit from the new way of eating."

The two walked down the Neonate Asylum hallway, but yelling from the outside courtyard stopped the woman in her tracks. She gazed out of the window to see a gathering crowd outside the perimeter gates. A voice over the intercom spoke to the audience outside.

"Innocent people are accused of being Addictors so that their children can be taken from them and used in production houses across the world. Selected SDTM's are programmed to give positive test results regardless of whether the individual has taken synthetic drugs or not.

Those Addictors who have poor genetic quality

are forcibly sterilized under the guise of having failed sobriety. Only those with excellent genetics are allowed to reproduce."

The woman gasped and raced towards the front room of the building, dragging the child along behind her. Other workers were frozen to their spots, listening in horror as their secrets were revealed.

"Who is that? Why haven't they been shut down?" the woman hissed.

"We can't tell, the voice is computer disguised. We can't even tell if it's male or female."

"Has anyone notified Ms. Winters?"

A young receptionist stared at the gaunt woman. "Do you really think she *doesn't* know about this by now? Half of the city is outside."

The voice continued. "Payment Repudiators are also innocent people who are used for their working capabilities and the prosperity of their land or creations. Once an individual acquires a certain level of success, they are removed from that equity so that the Dominion can keep the profits for themselves.

"In the event that they fight, their PIMs are either detonated under the guise of trying to escape or they are labeled as Repudiators and forcibly removed from their premises.

"Bernadette Winters is leading the Dominion

council in these practices and is now implementing a forced protocol for IV Infused Meal system. This protocol is under the cover of providing citizens of the Dominion healthy meal alternatives without having to scar the earth with the practice of growing food and raising animals for sustenance. What is contained in the IV's are the remnants of the deceased, both young and old. It also contains several bots which when engaged, can either kill you or infect you with a deadly virus. Your health will be in the hands of the Dominion government."

The crowd went silent for a moment before rage erupted. People began climbing the fences trying to get into the asylum and free the children.

"Daddy!" Inka screamed as she tugged at the hand that gripped onto hers.

The gaunt woman glanced out the glass doors and saw a determined and very angry looking man come charging towards the front doors. She yanked the child back to her as she ordered the receptionist to call the constabulary.

Inka kicked the woman hard in the shin and when she released her hand in pain, raced towards the glass doors and into her father's arms.

"Where's Jack Jr. baby?" Jack Sr. was sobbing as he stroked his daughter's hair.

"They took him somewhere last night, Daddy. I don't know where he is."

Jack Sr. ran back towards the toppling fencing and handed his daughter over to his wife. Sally grabbed their daughter and dropped to her knees, embracing her daughter tightly.

"Jack, find our baby boy," she whimpered.

He kissed her fiercely and then kissed the top of Inka's head before turning away and running back into the building. By this time the fence had toppled, and hoards of furious citizens were charging the brick building.

Sirens began to wail about the city speakers and a warning was announcing that people were to go back to their homes and check. Violators would have their PIMs detonated within thirty minutes. The voice was cut off and the nonbinary voice came over the intercom again.

"The programming for all citizen PIMs has been neutralized for the next twelve hours. Within that time, I encourage you to take back your lives before the Dominion over-rides the program again."

People cheered and began flooding the streets and attacking government buildings with any form of weaponry they could get their hands on. Constabulary were filing out of the CSS building wearing armor and face shields. They began beating some of the citizens down, attempting to force them back into their homes. The uprising had taken on a fever that even the militia couldn't cool.

Several of the citizens had climbed the trees and were hiding in the leaves, throwing rocks and other debris down onto the heads of the constabulary. Unable to defend themselves from the attack on the ground and in the trees, the soldiers began their retreat into the CSS building.

A large ACV came around the corner and began plowing over bodies, both citizen and constabulary alike. A raging scream came over the intercom of the ACV. "Die, all of you Vrana heathens, die!"

I gasped as I sat up, sweat dripping down my face. My pulse still raced in my veins and my limbs were weak and shaky as if I had been running in the streets.

I stumbled over to Finn and shook him. "Finn. Wake up! The Dominion, people are going to rise up."

Finn sat up and rubbed his hand over his face, trying to catch up with the words I was spewing. "What are you talking about, Willow?"

"I had a dream, like the one about the Crow's camp being attacked. Only this time it's going to happen behind Dominion walls. Someone tells everyone about the corruption of the government and there's a rebellion."

"When?"

I shook my head and closed my eyes, trying to remember any indication of the timeline. "Spring, late spring, I think. There are leaves on the trees. That's where a lot of citizens climb up to attack the soldiers."

"How does this help us?"

I shook my head. "It helps us in so many ways. It gives us more people who are willing to fight back, and it also means that we have someone on the inside who is aligned with our cause. We have an ally *inside* the Dominion."

"Did you see who?"

I frowned. "No. I don't even know if it's male or female. They disguised their voice when they took over the intercom and exposed the Dominion."

Finn took my hands in his. "Willow, it's great that the citizens of the Dominion are finally going to rise up but how does that help us? We have less than three-hundred Crows here. Even if almost all of the civilians rise up it won't be enough to stop the militia. They are armed and prepared. The citizens aren't, and not only do we *not* have enough weapons to outfit those citizens, we have no way of getting them there."

"We have more than three-hundred, Finn. We have the camp in Montana and who knows how many more scattered across the states. There has to be a way to get in touch will all of our members in the free zones," I argued, not willing to give up. "And if I can figure out who our ally is on the inside, we just may be able to smuggle in some weaponry before then."

"I don't know where the Montana camp is."

"But Duncan does and so does Dr. Stone."

"Willow, they've kept it secret from other Crows for a reason. To draw attention to it now would be dangerous."

"And the way we are living now isn't dangerous?" I stood up and placed my hands on my hips. "I'm done, Finn. We make a stand. We need to take our freedoms back for *everyone.*"

He stood up and placed his hands on my hips. I mentally dared him to argue with me right now; I was prepared to fight.

"Okay, you are right," he sighed. "But can we wait until morning? I don't think anyone would like to be awakened in the early morning hours."

I smiled up at him and nodded. "Dawn and no later."

He chuckled and wiped his face again. "Jeez, Willow. You can be exhausting, can't you?"

"It's one of my greater gifts."

TWELVE

IT WAS AFTER SEVEN WHEN everyone converged into the conference room. Voices hushed when I walked into the room with Finn and expectant eyes were focused on me. I didn't feel the fear or nervousness that I had before back at the other camp. I was surer of myself, and of my talents.

We made our way towards the front and Finn stepped back slightly to my side, letting everyone know that I was the one who was going to talk.

I smiled and shrugged my shoulders. "Sorry for getting everyone out of bed so early. You have to thank Finn because I wanted to get you all up before four this morning and he convinced me to wait until dawn."

My comment elicited chuckles, and I was relieved that they were receptive to being called at such an early hour. I continued. "I've been shown that there will be an uprising within the Dominion walls this spring. Citizens will be informed of the atrocities that have been plagued upon them and they will rebel. I think that we need to take this opportunity as a gift and help crush the Dominion oppressors."

Members began to talk animatedly between themselves, some shaking their heads no while others were nodding adamantly. I held up my hands for silence. "I believe we have an ally within the Dominion compound. They are the ones who enlighten the citizens of the Dominion's transgressions. If we can figure out who they are, they might be able to help us from the inside while we prepare. Maybe they can even prepare some citizens without attracting the attention of the constabulary."

"And how do you know all of this? Why should we risk all of this to free people who haven't helped themselves for the past eighteen years?"

I recognized Kathy's vicious tone and searched her out in the crowd. She tried to stay behind a larger man, but he stepped aside so I could face her directly. "For one, you should know by now that I sometimes have visions. It was one of these visions that saved the Crows from the last Dominion attack. And second, sometimes *stronger* and *braver* people need to aid those who are more helpless. To support them to rise and gain their freedom. Not all of us are born strong."

There were appreciative chuckles amongst the oldest members of the faction and I saw Kathy's face turn red. She stepped back, still glaring at me.

"I want word sent out to all of the factions scattered across the states. I want all of us to gather at the Montana camp by February."

"But that's only a couple months away," an older gentleman complained.

"Yes, it is so we need to send our swiftest and stealthiest members." I turned back to address the rest of the Crows. "As soon as Brice is healed, which Dr. Stone and Bradlee tell me should be the end of the week, I plan on traveling back with Dr. Stone to the Montana camp."

"Who's going to protect us, then?" Jennifer asked.

I chuckled. "Jennifer, I know for a fact you can protect yourself. And I promise that if I have any visions at all, I'll send word. But this faction has been looking out for each other for over seventeen years, I have faith you will stay by each other's sides and stay safe."

Duncan stood up and walked forward. "Willow, to be fair, it was less than six months ago that you showed up in our faction. My own son was the one who trained you. I know you have special gifts, but do you think you have the capabilities to take us into another war?"

I started to doubt myself, but my mother's voice rang in my mind. "You are a Falcon, Willow. Never forget that."

I cleared my throat. "I can't do this by myself, Duncan. With the technology you and your team have created and with which you have been able to counter the Dominion technology, that is what is going to give us the advantage. It's true, I have gifts and talents that I'm even today still discovering. Two months ago, we realized that I have the gift of visions and exceptional hearing. During my trip back into the Dominion compound I found out that I can see where the Dominion constables have been and what they were doing in the past. They come to me like blue ghosts, acting out their past actions."

I took a breath, unsure of if I should expose my latest two talents. I was on the fence on as to whether they would be accepted or not. I felt Finn grab my hand, offering his support. I glanced over at him and smiled my appreciation.

I turned back towards the faction and focused on Derek's image. "I also have the talent of making others see what I want."

I knew it was working because the men gasped, and many women screeched as Derek's mountainous form materialized before them. My voice had changed to his and my clothing became armored soldier's attire. I brought forth the soldier phantoms and had them wander through the crowd eliciting shrieks from those who came too close to an apparition.

I changed back into myself and waited for everyone to calm down. "This is what helped me get into the CSS after hours and rescue Brice."

I turned and searched for Bradlee. "We couldn't have escaped if it hadn't been for Bradlee's help. He released the Addictors and Payment Repudiators to create a distraction. He also gave us his truck so that we could make it to where we needed to meet up with Finn."

I took a deep breath. "And while I don't trust him one hundred percent, he helped me and Brice, and then he removed a tracker that had been lodged in my throat. He could've killed me, but he didn't."

I was shocked when Bradlee moved out from the crowd and stood beside me. He took my hand and I could tell he was seeking my strength. He was shaking so hard that I was surprised my body didn't tremble with his shudders. I felt Finn step back from me, but I didn't have a chance to address it because I felt over two hundred eyes watching expectantly.

Bradlee cleared his throat. "I'll admit I was sent here to spy on the Crows and to expose your weaknesses but while I was here, I saw how you all live and interact. Every person is important and every person has a voice. I'd never experienced that before and after I went back to the Dominion with Brice, I realized my mistake. I want to prove to all of you that I'm worthy of being a part of you and that I will never betray you again."

There were murmurs amongst the crowd and I wasn't sure if he had convinced everyone. He would definitely have to prove himself.

"So with all of that information, I plan on leaving in seven days' time. That will give me the time to prepare, for us to send out our fastest scouts to take messages to our fellow faction leaders and Brice to heal. When Dr. Stone leaves to go back to Montana, I plan on going with him."

I exited the front of the building so that I could go see my brother. I had a lot to do to prepare for my trip. I had never been to another state; the Dominion kept their people close to home.

I heard footsteps come up behind me and I turned to face Bradlee.

"I wanted to talk to you about something," he leaned over as if out of breath, but I knew him to be in better shape than that. He was stalling to organize his words; a blind man could see that.

"What is it, Bradlee?"

"I want to come with you to Montana."

I snorted and walked away, heading towards the infirmary. "Fat chance of that ever happening."

"Willow, please, hear me out. I can help you up there. Better than I can here," he was jogging along trying to keep up with my extended pace.

"Out of the question, Bradlee. I still don't trust you, and the Dominion is chomping at the bit to get the Crow's Montana location. Isn't it just convenient that you want to go and that you…" I turned and faced him, raising my hands up in air quotes. "can help us up there. No, absolutely not." I continued my march.

"Think about it, Willow. They have advanced technology not only in medical but in IT. Technology that even the Dominion hasn't thought of."

I turned and studied him. "And how do you know this?"

"Jason told me," he waved his hands. "Not

everything. He doesn't trust me either but after I healed you and he saw the progress on Brice, he's starting to. He thinks that I can help break some codes they've been struggling with. That a fresh pair of eyes might see a solution that they are too close to see."

"I'll talk to Jason. I'm not convinced, Bradlee. You betrayed us before and there are even higher risks this time. I'm not sure I'm open to making that gamble." I moved on.

"I'll put a tracker in or a Crow PIM. You can hold the detonator. If I betray you or the faction or do anything suspicious, you have the power of ending me."

I stopped walking again and studied his face. If he wasn't sincere, he was an excellent actor. Of course, I had bought his gig many months ago, hadn't I? But if we truly could install a tracker or a device, maybe he could be trusted? I dropped my head and stared at the ground. "I'll think about it, Bradlee. I'll give you my answer in a couple days. That's the best I can offer."

He nodded excitedly. "That's all I ask for," he grinned widely and rushed in and kissed me quickly on the cheek. "Thank you, Willow. You won't be sorry." He rushed off to his cabin and I found his smile infectious.

"You are trusting him now?"

I turned and found Finn standing on the side of the

smokehouse. I shrugged my shoulders. "I don't think I would use the word trust, but he's willing to put into place guarantees that would make it safer for us to give him a chance."

"He'll manipulate those just as easy as he's manipulated you."

I felt my neck bristle. "You think I'm easy to manipulate? Since when, Finnian Sennet?"

He blew out his breath and walked towards me. "You've changed, Willow"

He attempted to take my hands, but I pulled them out of his reach. "Yes, I have changed. Going through everything I have the past six months tends to change a person. And I'm sure I'm going to continue changing as events unfold."

"But you've changed a *lot*."

My now too frequent emotion of anger rose up in my body. "And you didn't change a lot after the betrayal of your mother? After her loss and the loss of half of your faction?" I felt the anger building. "That's so unfair, Finn. You can change because of the circumstances in your life; *life altering events*, yet you expect me to stay the same, naïve innocent Willow who showed up at camp back in October? Well screw you, Finnian. If you don't like me now, then you can just move on. I hear Kathy has the hots for you. Maybe she will be your constant."

I stomped off hating how the conversation had turned so rapidly and how I handled the situation. My words were meant to inflict pain and I'm sure I did that, but was it what I really wanted? No, but my pride wasn't going to let me go back and apologize.

I took a deep breath. I wasn't completely in the wrong either. It wasn't fair of Finnian to expect me *not* to change. He knew of the losses I had sustained. He knew I was learning new talents and how to handle them; talents that others didn't have. How could I experience all of these new things and *not* be changed?

I reached the infirmary house and paused at the door. I didn't want to bring all of my negative emotions into the room with Brice. He was still dealing with all of his baggage and I didn't need to add my own.

Shaking my head to clear it, I opened the door with a smile on my face. The smile turned to shock as I saw Brice sitting up and sipping clear fluids. Jason turned to see who had come in, and when he saw my expression, grinned madly.

"Isn't it incredible? Bradlee has knowledge that will be beneficial to all of us. His technique has decreased Brice's healing time almost five hundred percent."

I walked over to Brice who was attempting to

smile. The damaged side of his face was still slack but the twinkle in his eyes showed me he was happy with the progress too.

I tentatively touched the new skin, as fresh and smooth as a newborn child. "This is incredible."

Jason came up beside me. "He still needs to be careful. No solid foods. If he were to accidently bite down on the new flesh, it would tear and reopen the hole. But it's filled in enough that he can enjoy liquids. The muscle contains more mass and fibers so it's slower to grow in than the skin is but already you can see the outline through the skin where the muscle is coming in."

I stared at the faint bulge around the soft flesh. I could definitely tell that the hole circumference was getting smaller. I threw my arms around Brice, spilling some of his broth. "This is wonderful, Brice! What a miracle!"

I leaned back and saw tears streaming down Brice's face. I could feel his happiness mixed with the pain and sorrow. He hadn't had time to grieve the loss of our parents or deal with the pain of torture that he had been put through. I couldn't even imagine the horrors he endured and still didn't betray his faction. I always knew my big brother was strong, I just hadn't realized *how* strong. "I love you so much,

Brice. So much stuff is happening. The Dominion aren't taking care of their people. The government is filled with liars and betrayers to get what they want and the citizens are just pawns in their game to be used for strategy then tossed away," I wiped my own eye to clear it from the moisture that had gathered. "They are torturing little kids, Brice. Tearing families apart without any care or concern. I saw it with my own eyes, and it needs to stop."

I leaned closer to his ear, wanting this part of the conversation to be heard only by my brother's ear. "I had a vision last night. Like the one I had about the camp being attacked. There's an uprising coming, Brice. The citizens are going to learn the truth by an insider who takes over the government announcement system. The people will learn what their leaders are really like and a reckoning will happen. We need to be there to help them. To take down those forces once and for all."

I pulled back and stared into his eyes. I saw encouragement and determination, but I also saw fear. I stroked the side of his face. "You don't need to go. Duncan is going to need your expertise with the new trackers we found and hopefully more ACVs."

He frowned slightly and shook his head. "Tweee."

I giggled as the tears slipped down my cheek.

"Don't worry about me, you goof. I'm going to be fine and stop calling me Tree. You know I hate that nickname."

He smiled again, his stroke-like appearance tugging at my heart. I had missed him so much.

Jason cleared his throat and stepped forward. "Willow. I was hoping to talk with you for a minute if you have the time."

I ruffled Brice's hair as I stood up, knowing how much he hated it but wasn't fast enough to stop me. I turned towards Jason. "Yep. I have time now."

He indicated that he wanted to talk in the surgical room, so I stepped through and walked over to the table where I had lain earlier.

"I know that Bradlee has betrayed the faction and is actually a citizen of the Dominion. I also know he has the knowledge that could help advance our medical abilities and technology. Bradlee has suggested we insert an explosive tracking device, similar to a PIM. As an alternative, I was even thinking we could have a neck collar installed."

"Have you contacted your members up in Montana? What do they think of bringing a known spy into the camp that you have worked so hard to keep hidden?" I was feeling slightly irritated.

Jason flushed slightly and looked away for a

moment. "We kept it hidden to protect the largest faction of the Crows. At the time, we were the most advanced society in the free-zone."

"And you didn't think that you would help your fellow constituents? You'd leave us out to fend for ourselves?

He shook his head. "No, it wasn't like that. We knew if we gathered everyone together it would garner the attention of the Dominion and their constabulary. We couldn't risk that."

"You're just as bad as the Dominion. You were choosing who would benefit and who could be sacrificed."

"I'm not explaining myself very well. We just needed time. We have been preparing so that when the time comes to rise again, the Conformists will win and the Dominion will fall," he placed a hand on my shoulder. "When you come with us you will see. We haven't forgotten the other brothers and sisters of our faction."

I blew out a breath and looked out the sealed-up window. I felt like I was fighting with everyone today. Maybe I was the one who had the problem. Maybe I had a chip on my shoulder that I was itching for someone to knock off. "Okay, Jason. We will take Bradlee with us. He will have a neck collar on or another device that we all agree on. I won't leave another camp exposed like ours was."

"Fantastic! I will talk with him now and we will figure out the best device to accommodate all of our needs."

I stepped back through the doorway and smiled at Brice before leaving the infirmary. I needed to be alone and clear my head. I couldn't stop my chuckle at my own irony. I spent the past week alone behind the Dominion walls counting the minutes until I'd be back with the Crows yet here I was, trying to get away. I honestly made no sense.

I turned east from the camp and picked a trail that wasn't as worn as the others were. It gave me a greater chance of not being disturbed. Hadn't my mom always told me that the path less travelled can make all of the difference? She was always bringing up quotes from books and poems she had studied in college. One of her other passions besides art.

The trail wound around a small hill before dropping down into a steep ravine. It reminded me of Angel Falls except there was no river or waterfall at the bottom. Just acres and acres of trees. I glanced up to try and see the tops of the evergreens that loomed above the leafless cousins below. Though the sun was out without a cloud in the sky, the air was brisk and cold. I realized we were getting close to the time that Mom insisted we celebrate Grandma's favorite holiday. Thanksgiving.

"It's a time to come together as family, regardless of blood, and find thanks for all of the blessings both big and small that come into our lives."

I remember her spouting this every year before the end of November and Grandma saying the exact same words before she passed. Family and blood. Blessings and thanks. Had any of us really stopped to think about how far we'd come?

I found a break in the trees that allowed a patch of sunshine down to the earth below. I sat on a stone, absorbing what little heat it still held. It was cold and I hadn't dressed to be outdoors for this long, but I didn't want to go back yet. I still needed to find answers for all of the things that troubled me.

"You are so quick to judge but expect others to be patient with your learning."

I whirled and saw my grandmother standing in the shadows.

"How..."

"I'm a Falcon, too, Willow. It doesn't skip a generation, only a gender."

I glanced at the ground and nodded. "I'm trying to be patient but it seems like every time I make a decision it offends or bothers someone else. I just can't seem to make everyone happy."

She chuckled and stepped closer. "That's the challenge of being a leader. You will never make everyone happy. It's impossible. You have to trust in yourself and your leadership. You need to make the tough decisions based on the knowledge that *you* have that others might not be privy to. Leave the smaller, more insignificant decisions to others. It helps them feel like they are still a part of your band, your faction."

"So, I need to let others decide how to deal with Bradlee and focus on the bigger picture?"

"That's one of them, but you need to decide the kind of woman you want to be. Will you be solitary and cold, or will you share your life and decisions with another and choose a life partner? You can't have it both ways."

I eyed her critically. "You're talking about Finn, aren't you?"

"You can't expect him to be involved with your life only when you want him to. Partnerships don't work that way. You either need to embrace all of this relationship, good and bad, or walk away. It's not fair to either one of you, otherwise."

"Yeah but he's accusing me of changing which of *course* I'm changing. I've had major things happen to me and they've left wounds that haven't healed yet."

"And you don't think he's experienced the same thing?"

"I know he has with his mother, and feeling like he's disappointed his father, but he doesn't have the gifts that I do, or the stress of figuring out how they work and what they do."

"No but he has the gift of loving someone unconditionally despite them pushing him away repeatedly. Let him in, Willow. Communicate and share with him. Or let him go."

"Was it that way with Mom and Dad, too? Did she let Dad in?"

"The relationship between your mother and father was complicated and very different from the one you have with Finn. You can't compare the two."

I sighed. "What happened, Grandma? Why did Dad betray us and the faction?"

"He was pulled by routine and compliancy. Change is difficult but always inevitable. Nothing can stay the same, regardless of how hard you fight it."

"But he tried to kill me. His own daughter."

"Things aren't always what they seem, Willow. Sometimes you have to dig a little deeper below the surface to see the truth."

I shook my head. "What does that even mean? I *saw* him and heard the words that were coming out of his mouth. I know the truth."

She started to shimmer away and I stood quickly, reaching out to stop her from leaving.

"Always seek the truth, Willow. Even if you think you already know what it is."

"Grandma. What does all of that mean?"

"Am I interrupting something?"

I whirled and saw Finn standing at the trail. "No, not anymore."

He turned to leave. "I'm sorry, I didn't mean to interrupt."

"No! Don't go. You didn't interrupt. She was leaving anyway."

He took a hesitant step towards me. "Your mother?"

I smiled. "No. Grandma this time."

"Wow. Have you been able to talk to all of your family?"

"No. I haven't talked to my father," I shrugged. "I don't know that I really want to."

He blew out a breath and sat down on a stone next to mine. "I get that. I don't know that I would ever want to talk to my mom. Though it might be good to get some answers."

"Did you ever talk to Duncan about it?"

"Kinda, but not really. He started to explain things, but I got angry and shouted over him once he told me he had known for a while that she was a turncoat." He threw a stone out into the grass. "We didn't talk about it anymore after that. We don't really talk about anything."

He threw another stone and glanced up at me. "That's how I feel about us, Willow."

I frowned, his words feeling harsh. "We talk, Finn."

"No, we don't," he shook his head. "Not since you got back. We talk, but we don't talk about anything important. You *tell* me what you want to do and how the faction is going to proceed but there's no back and forth involved at all. Sometimes it feels like you don't need me anymore. Not even as a friend."

I released the pent-up air I held in my lungs. "I do need you, Finn. I need you as a friend and so much more. You were the first person who believed in me besides my mother and I'll never forget that."

"But you don't feel that way towards me anymore. You like Bradlee."

I jerked my head and stared at him. "What? Bradlee? I'm not interested in Bradlee."

"It looks that way from my perspective. You are

quick to defend him and you two appear to have shared a lot of history in the short time you were gone."

I opened my mouth to argue but shut it quickly, trying to see it from Finn's perspective. If the shoe were on the other foot, I could see why Finn thought what he did. I nodded and stared at the grass at my feet. "I can see why you think that. I guess I'm empathetic to him. I know what it's like growing up within the Dominion's Collectivism. Granted my parents told me about the Crows and what freedom was but I was still raised under the day to day oppression of the Dominion."

"So, you have things in common."

"Yes, we do but that doesn't mean I'm into him. I just understand where he's coming from." I gently grabbed Finn's hand. "And if it wasn't for his help, Finn, Brice and I wouldn't have escaped the CSS building. He *lied* to Aurysia and his brother to lead them in another direction to buy us time. Then he released all of the hostages and kept the constabulary busy gathering them all back up."

I took a deep breath trying to put together the words that would explain how I felt about Bradlee. "People change; people *can* change. Your mother and my father did; it was just for the worst. I think

Bradlee is wanting to change but change for the better. Why can't we give him a chance as long as we are cautious?"

"We can and you are right. People can change. I'm just wary of those who change so quickly."

"It might not be quickly in his mind. He might have been doubting the Dominion for a long time and we just didn't see it." I squeezed his hand. "And as far as you and I go. I need you, Finn. I know that I haven't been as open or communicative as I should've been but all of that changes now. I still have so much to learn, and I have no idea if there are still other gifts that are yet to present themselves to me. I need someone who is patient with me and will call me out when I'm being ridiculous, closed off or full of myself. I never want to forget who I am."

He stared at me, his green eyes never leaving mine and I knew he was struggling with something inside of himself. As I had asked for patience from him, I needed to have patience *for* him.

"I'm not sure how patient I can be with Bradlee and I won't lie; I'm jealous as hell when I see him with you, but I'll try. I'll try for you, Willow."

He leaned over and kissed me softly. I closed my eyes, wanting more but I felt him shiver.

"We need to get back before both of us get sick."

He nodded and kissed me quickly. "I'm sure Bradlee has a cure for that, too."

"Finn."

He held up his hands. "Sorry. Won't happen again."

I laughed as I stood up and grabbed his hand. We stepped onto the trail and slowly began to make our way back to the camp. I wanted to talk to him about my conversation with Grandma, but I wasn't sure how to. Some of her comments felt cryptic and I wasn't sure if I could communicate them accurately.

I decided to leave it for another time and have the conversation I was dreading to have. "Jason is thrilled with Brice's recovery and has no doubt at all that he will be completely healed before it's time to leave for Montana."

"Yep. I went and saw Brice last night and was amazed at the progress. Bradlee and Dr. Stone seem to work well together."

"Yeah…"

"Spit it out, Willow. You said you wanted to be more open and communicative. Let's start now and I'll help. You are going to Montana with Bradlee and Dr. Stone and you want me here to lead our faction."

I jerked at his accuracy. I don't know why I felt like I was betraying him but maybe a part of me was. I was leaving him again to go to another place.

"I get it. It makes sense. Someone needs to be here to make sure all of our supplies and ammunition are loaded and ready for movement. I'm the head of the Scout team so naturally it should be me." He stopped me and pulled me in front of him. "I'll do this as you want but promise me, you'll be safe. Talk to me whenever you can and keep me in the loop of things that are going on; both with you and around you."

I smiled and threw my arms around his neck. He squeezed me tightly to him and I knew the closest thing to peace that I had felt since my parent's death. "I promise, Finn. From here on out I will tell you everything and we will keep this faction safe, together."

"That's all I ask, Will."

THIRTEEN

"JUST A PAIN IN THE A..."

"Brice! Don't call your sister bad names," Jennifer chastised.

"Don't waste your breath, Jennifer. He's been a crude jerk all of his life," I laughed as Brice punched me in the arm.

"Don't make me hurt you, Tree."

"Ugh. Stupid nicknames. What is it with guys coming up with the most annoying nicknames? You use Tree, Derek was calling me Vrana, whatever that means. Enough! If you are going to call me a name, call me something cool."

The giggling stopped and I saw Jennifer staring at me, her face pale.

"What's wrong? What did I say?"

She swallowed hard, "Vrana is the Czech name for crow."

I shook my head, not understanding why she was so upset. "I told you, they knew I was coming. He was just calling me out to let me know he knew I was a Crow is all."

She glanced at Brice who was watching her intensely before looking back at me. "You are right, I forgot they knew."

Brice and I faced each other, both of us shrugging at the same time.

"Are you all packed for your upcoming journey, little sister?"

"Yep. I think I have all of my stuff packed into Bernice. Jason and Bradlee have their OHV loaded and ready to go," I grabbed an apple off of the breakfast bar and polished it on the sleeve of my sweater. "I think Joni is going too."

Brice cleared his throat. "Oh, Joni is going to Montana? Why is she doing that?"

"Oh, I think she's interested in the medical advancements Montana has," I was trying to figure out if the hole in my apple was from a worm or not when the tone in his voice dawned on me. I turned to face him. "You like her, don't you?"

His face flushed, the new flesh on his cheek slightly lighter than the rest of his face. "Pfft, no, I was just wondering if…"

"You like Joni! You like Joni!" I sang, laughing as he stood up and lunged towards me. I quickly ducked his advancement and placed the dining table between us. "Should I say something to her?"

His face blanched and he waved his hands. "No, Willow. God please don't say anything."

I stopped moving when he did and stared at him. "Wow, you *really* like her. I swear Brice, I won't say anything to her as long as you promise to say something to her before we go."

"Like what? What am I supposed to say to her?"

"Ask her if she's excited or nervous about going to Montana. Ask her what she thinks about the medical advancements of Montana and whether she thinks it will help our faction or not."

He shook his head. "What if she doesn't like me?"

I moved around the table and punched him in the arm. "Geez Brice, always going to the dark side. What if she *does* like you and you never say anything and then she goes off and falls in love with some tech or medical guy up in Montana and you spend your life as a sad bachelor, mourning the girl you didn't have the guts to say anything to."

I giggled at his expression. His eyes were wide as the story I just told played out in his head. My brother may be older but he sure was easy.

"You are right. I'll go talk to her now."

"Brice, it's eight o'clock in the morning. You might be a little intense for her this early. Why don't you wait for the party tonight? Things will be a little more laid back and sociable."

"And you can ease your nerves with a drink. That's what my David did when we first started talking," Jennifer offered.

"Yeah, that always helps. Liquid courage," Brice agreed.

"Just don't have so much liquid courage that you botch it up," I pointed out. I stood up on my tiptoes and kissed him on the cheek. "I've got to go and make sure all the loose ends are tied up. I'll see you tonight, bro."

"See you tonight, Willow."

I kicked through the fluffy snow that had fallen two nights before and made my way down to Bernice. I had clothes, my bow and quiver packed, and several rifles stowed within the machine. I still wasn't very good with guns but as Finn had pointed out, I wouldn't get better if I didn't practice.

I turned on the machine and went through a

last-minute check of all the gauges. I didn't want any issues when we left in the morning. Everything checked fine and I shut the engine down. I was ready to go…physically.

I climbed back out of Bernice and headed towards the bat cave. The nickname had stuck when others heard of it and now everyone was calling it that. I knew Finn would be there training scouts. I walked in and noticed the immediate temperature difference. It was at least forty degrees warmer and the windows dripped with the humidity in the air. Grunts and hits permeated the air and I stood back to watch the two fighters in the ring.

One was Kathy, a smug smile on her face and the other was Finn, his face emotionless and still. She lunged towards him to hit him at his waist, but he spun at the last minute, causing her to trip and fall forward with her momentum. She hit the mat with a grunt but sprang up quickly, whirling to face him.

"Pretty smooth, Finnian, but wait until I have you underneath me."

I hated the insinuation and I knew it was intentional, so I cleared my throat. Kathy turned sharply to face me as Finn took the opportunity to lunge forward and drop her to the mat.

He loomed over her, a frown on his face. "Don't let *anyone* distract you; ever."

Kathy propped herself up on her elbow, staring at him. "But she..."

"She did nothing that the enemy won't do. There are distractions everywhere. You need to focus on your enemy."

She threw a glare in my direction. "I will from now on."

He held his hand out to help her up and she took it eagerly. I almost threw up in my mouth when I heard her giggle as she flung herself close to him like he had pulled her up too powerfully.

He stepped away from her and stepped through the ropes, making his way towards me. He wrapped his arm around my waist and pulled me in for a kiss. It wasn't the peck expected. It was packed with heat as he nibbled my bottom lip. When he finally released me, I saw Kathy glaring at us over his shoulder. I pulled back and searched his eyes for an explanation.

"Now nobody should have any question where my intentions lie."

I nodded my head. "Nope, no question at all."

He stepped back and began to unwrap his hands. "Are you packed and ready to go?"

I nodded. "Yep. Just got done checking Bernice

and everything is in working order." I pulled him off to the side so Kathy's eavesdropping ears wouldn't hear. "I've been thinking about it. Why don't you come with us? Quinn is super smart and been with the Crows almost as long as you have. He could handle it here."

Finn chuckled. "Quinn? He panics when he has to decide what color underwear he should choose in the morning. I can't leave the faction in Quinn's hands."

"What about Derant? He's very decisive and could handle any problems that should arise."

"Willow. What is this really about? Why the change of heart?"

I shook my head. "I've been thinking about it and you are right. We need to be honest and open and work together and how can we work together when we are in separate states? We are good together; powerful together. It doesn't make any sense for us to be apart."

"It does, for right now. You are right. We are both smart and powerful. We need to be strong now for our factions and lead them to success. Whatever secrets Montana holds, you need to discover and figure out how it's going to help us with the uprising," he stroked my hair. "It won't be a long separation, but it is necessary."

I closed my eyes. I knew he was right, but it still felt wrong to me. I opened my eyes and looked at him. "Are we still going to the farewell party tonight?"

"Of course we are. I want to dance with my lady."

I smiled and kissed him quickly. "Okay, I'll see you tonight."

"See you tonight."

"Sweetheart, I wanted you to have this. I made it for you after your mother passed. I know it's not much, but I needed to do something. She was one of my best friends."

I took the elegant fabric from her hands and held out the dress. It wasn't as beautiful as my mother's prom dress but it was close. The black, silky material shimmered in the light and deep purple lace covered the exposed, deep V line in the back; the point almost reaching the small of my back. I smiled at her and pulled her in to hug her.

"It's absolutely gorgeous, Jennifer. I will wear it tonight."

"I guessed on the size though you seem to be the same as your mother, just a wee bit shorter."

"I'm sure it will fit perfect. Thank you again."

"Thank you, sweet Willow. You are such a blessing

to our group, and I know you have the best intentions for our future. We are trusting you to lead us into the life we've been missing for so many years. There are still many of us who remember what freedom tastes like."

"I know I have never experienced it, I listened to Mom and Dad talk about it so I *think* I know what it will be like and I'm looking forward to that time."

"You and me both. Now go get ready so you can knock that boy's socks off."

I giggled and hugged her again. "Thank you. I will."

I made my way back to my cabin and opened the door tentatively. I didn't want Finn to see me before the party. When I found the room empty, I slipped into the bathroom and quickly cleaned up. I released my hair from its braid and brushed it out, the waves shimmering in the light from the tight weave it had been bound in all day. I slipped on the dress and turned so that my back was facing the mirror. I had been right; Jennifer had sized it perfectly and it fit like a glove.

I waited for thirty minutes before heading to the commons central where the party was being held. It used to be an old hay barn before the war, but the Crows had converted it into a place to gather and stay out of the weather. Because of its tall, vaulted ceiling, it was easy to build fires within to help warm the interior without the risk of carbon monoxide poisoning.

Despite it only being short of five in the evening, it was already dark outside. Thankfully there were lanterns to light the path so I wouldn't trip on unseen objects. I slipped inside and stayed to the outside wall. I had always felt more comfortable being able to ascertain my surroundings before I actually participated. It was one of the ways I was able to build confidence in unknown situations.

I saw several people dancing in the center of the building on the makeshift dancefloor. Quinn and Joni were twisting and twirling like they had been dance partners for years. I caught Brice over by the drink table watching them closely. He almost appeared to be pouting.

Kathy and Evander were dancing though their tempo was slower and they appeared deep in conversation. Occasionally Kathy would glance over in the opposite corner, something there holding her attention. I glanced over and wasn't surprised to see Finn there talking with Jason Stone. He appeared to be oblivious to Kathy's attentions.

"Staking out the barn?"

I jumped and whirled, the back hem of my dress

catching on my heels and throwing me off balance. I felt myself falling and then I felt Bradlee's large arms catch me before I hit the floor. He pulled me back upright and grinned. "I've never had a lady fall for me before."

I felt my face flush and pushed away from him. The last thing I needed was for what just happened to be misconstrued. I glanced over at Finn who was still talking to Jason. Thank god he hadn't seen that.

"I didn't *fall* for you, Bradlee. You startled me and caused me to trip."

"Now that doesn't sound as nice, does it?"

"It's the truth and I won't allow you to twist it into any other way," I turned towards Finn. "Now if you'll excuse me, I'm needed over there."

"Save me a dance, Willow."

I didn't turn or acknowledge him, but I saw Finn look up when he heard Bradlee's voice. I could feel his eyes eat me up and noticed he was no longer listening to Jason. When Jason realized he had lost his audience, he searched for Finn's distraction; his mouth dropping slightly when he saw me.

He closed his mouth and grinned, patting Finn on the shoulder and saying something to him. Finn nodded and made his way towards me. We met in the middle of the room and he smiled at me.

"You look absolutely stunning, Willow."

"Thank you, Finnian. Jennifer made the dress for me."

"She did an excellent job."

"Yes, she did." I glanced around the room and noticed we had gained the attention of some of the others. "Do you want to get something to eat or drink?"

"No, I want to dance with my lady. Willow, will you dance with me?"

I accepted his hand and we moved to the middle of the dance floor. I didn't see anyone else, only Finn and when the music slowed, he pulled me in close. I rested my head on his shoulder. I could hear his heartbeat and its steady beat soothed my soul. I wanted to remember every moment of this night because those memories would keep me company while I was in Montana. I didn't know how long I was going to be there or how long Finn and I were going to be apart. I was leaving my family again to keep the larger family safe; a family I had been a part of for just a fraction of my life but just as bound as any blood.

"What are you thinking, Willow?"

I sighed; my thoughts disrupted. "I was thinking that I want to remember every smell, sensation, and taste from tonight to carry me through the lonely nights. I was thinking how odd that this group of people has become my family, though I didn't even know them a year ago. I was thinking that I don't want to leave your arms and I want you to hold me until we are old and gray."

"I wish it were that easy."

I nodded on his shoulder, the silky material of his shirt caressing my cheek.

"Come with me." He pulled me off of the dance floor and outside.

I shivered at the sudden difference in temperature but kept up with him. He took us back to our cabin, releasing my hand as he knelt to the floor and pulled something out from underneath his cot. He placed the wrapped object on his bed and looked up at me.

"I had this made for you."

"What is it?"

He stood up and pointed towards the bundle. "Open it and find out."

I moved towards his bed and unwrapped the blanket to expose a beautiful broadsword. The long silver blade glimmered in the lamp light. I picked it up and caressed the hilt, a purple moonstone sparkled with each movement. I turned towards Finn. "It's gorgeous, Finn."

"Yes, Jessie did an excellent job."

"Jessie, from the scout team?"

"Yep, the one and only. He dabbles in silver and blacksmithing and when I approached him with this project, he was eager to take it on." He moved towards me and kissed my lips. "I want you to keep it with you always for protection. It's enchanted, your hands are the only ones to wield it."

"I promise, I'll keep it safe." I smiled up at him. "Please reconsider, Finn? Come with me."

He chuckled and brushed the tip of my nose with his finger. "No Willow. We've already been through this. We need to put the faction first. Now let's get back to the party before they send a scout team looking for us. I know Brice was building the confidence to ask Joni to dance and I believe our little Quinn asked permission for a dance with my lady."

"Okay, but know I won't give up asking," I teased as I wrapped the sword back into the blanket. I placed it carefully on my cot before taking Finn's hand and walking back towards the barn.

Tonight was the last night I would be with this group of people before the Rising. There were believers and non-believers; those who loved me and those who hated me but all of them chose to follow me. Tonight, we were coming together as a band of

Crow; a murder was the term. When we would come together again it would no longer be as Crows. The next time we joined forces it would be for the Rise of Falcons.

~THE END~

Thank you so much for reading Willow's second tale, Flight of Sparrows. She will continue her saga with Rise of Flacons, coming out March 26th, 2021. Want to know how the Dominion got their power and how this all started? Stay tuned for Declaration of Crows, the prequel of the Small Sacrifices Series releasing May 21, 2021.

You can reach me at www.raeannehadley.com or email me at raeannehadley@hotmail.com.

Thank you again!

Made in the USA
Columbia, SC
04 November 2021